CLEVER BY HALF

CLEVER BY HALF

Learning and Loving in a Fifties University

Donald Read

Book Guild Publishing
Sussex, England

First published in Great Britain in 2012 by
The Book Guild Ltd
Pavilion View
19 New Road
Brighton, BN1 1UF

Typesetting in Baskerville by
Nat-Type, Cheshire

Printed and bound in Great Britain by
CPI Group (UK) Ltd, Croydon, CR0 4YY

A catalogue record for this book is available from
The British Library.

ISBN 978 1 84624 783 5

FOR KATE

Who was a student there!

'Autumn gathers round and a new batch of students are here; one's colleagues are back, seeming more dingy, more of a personal humiliation than before even to *see*, let alone *be with* and EQUAL TO.'

Philip Larkin, 21 October 1958

'I recall being told that a university Faculty generally comprises mistrustful and jealous egocentrics who are forced together by the common need for car parking.'

Professor Mark Hill, QC, *The Times*, 17 March 2011

Contents

1

New Beginnings

(1)

'Damn Mellors! What's he up to now?' The Professor of History, Andrew Grey, was talking to a colleague about the Professor of English. 'He's trying to do us down! He wants more lecture theatre time. He's always wanting to be top dog!'

His colleague nodded in regretful agreement. 'Ah, yes. A pity. Literature used to be a subject for ladies and gentlemen. Not now. Not here.'

'Sometimes I feel I could hit him. Even when he isn't plotting, he's smearing our good name. I may have to speak to the Dean.'

Harsh words. But was this merely a passing spat? Or something likely to have unhappy consequences? We shall see. Universities are like volcanoes – superficially calm, but rumbling beneath; and liable to intermittent molten eruptions.

Despite these personal tensions, this was a hopeful time for Blackchester. It was a small 'civic' university. And this was the 1950s. The very label 'civic university' had only recently been popularised.

Such places had been founded during the previous hundred years as local second-bests to Oxford, Cambridge and London. These three older universities still reigned supreme, but the larger civics had progressed steadily enough down the years – Manchester and the like. On the other hand, the smaller institutions – in places such as Leicester or Exeter – had developed more uncertainly. They had remained as what were called 'university colleges'. They conducted their own teaching, but had accepted that their degrees must be awarded through the University of London.

Blackchester had been one of these lesser unpretentious colleges. Not well known. But then at last came the breakthrough. In 1953, as part of the expansion of higher education after the Second World War, it had been made into a full university, able to award its own degrees.

University expansion was a sign that the country was at last regaining confidence. Labour's 'welfare state', which had come into being straight after the war, had been introduced defiantly against the odds: this Conservative initiative came later and was more temperate.

What then would Blackchester's new status mean for the lives of those who worked there – for its teachers and taught, for its support staff? Professors, lecturers, secretaries, students. How much better, or how much worse? We shall see.

There were still only about eleven hundred students on the Blackchester campus, but the target was a tripling of these numbers within a few years. Currently, the Arts Faculty had about six hundred students, Social Science three hundred and Natural Science two hundred. All these young people wanted university degrees so as to get good jobs, and most of them were the first members of their families to reach university. Even so, only about a quarter came from working-class homes. Most Blackchester students were more or less middle-class – with a greater proportion from the lower-middle than was the case at more prestigious universities. Many spoke with mild regional accents, although this was stronger when they first came than when they left. Just a few, usually with strong left-wing opinions, made a point of retaining their local accents to the end.

Most Blackchester students only half understood their university's new status; they simply noted that their degrees would now be awarded by 'Blackchester' instead of by 'London'.

(2)

Blackchester did not yet teach applied science or medicine, but the hope was that these important subjects would be added at some future date, after major investment. Meanwhile, the plan was to expand existing departments year-by-year, especially on the Arts side. The Blackchester professors and lecturers now had a rare chance to achieve academic excellence widely and quickly.

Could they do it? Not all of them. In a private letter, the Blackchester librarian had recently described his academic colleagues as, overall, 'a cabinet of mediocrities'. He was a rising literary figure whose own fame was destined to cast reflected glory upon the university. He tended to gloomy exaggeration. But certainly on the science side Blackchester's senior Professors were mostly exhausted volcanoes: they had been appointed in the 1930s as young men of promise, and had then become trapped at Blackchester because they had not lived up to that promise. The senior Professor of Chemistry had not published an academic paper since 1938.

In contrast, English and History were already becoming known nationally as lively departments. Obscure but worthy provincial secondary schools sent them some of their better pupils each year. Professor Daniel Mellors, Blackchester's English Professor, was an authority upon nineteenth-century British novelists. Professor Andrew Grey, the History

Professor, was an expert on nineteenth-century British politics.

The two men had more in common than the historical period in which they specialised. Both were in their late thirties. Both came from lower-middle-class families. Both had been scholarship boys at provincial grammar schools – Mellors in Birmingham, Grey in Leeds. They had each then won scholarships to Oxford.

Almost inevitably, their origins and progress had required them to be aspiring characters. And yet their similarity of background and their related research interests had not brought them into close accord at Blackchester. On the contrary, they were rivals on campus. Contact between the two men was cool. While Grey privately called Mellors 'big-headed', Mellors called Grey 'tricky'.

Both had been appointed in the same year, 1948, when the two founding professors in their subjects had retired. Why had Mellors and Grey chosen to come to Blackchester at all? Each knew that they were taking a career risk in moving to such a humble place in the academic pecking order; but they were arrogant enough to believe that they could make a mark there which would be noticed within the wider university world. They had both fled in their early thirties from lectureships at big civic universities because they were tired of being stifled by the hierarchical structures at such places. So they had moved to Blackchester – but not for life.

In just one respect Blackchester was undoubtedly superior to the big civics. These larger universities were housed in smoke-grimed buildings close to noisy city centres. Blackchester, in contrast, stood on a broad green campus at the edge of town. Its original teaching buildings had been built between the wars in a mild art-deco style, which had worn well both stylistically and physically. The English and History departments were housed in the two-storied Arts building, which dated from 1928.

As befitted the principal subjects within their Faculty, both departments were located in prime positions on the ground floor – History on the left as you went in, English on the right. 'We are always on the right side,' was a quip frequently used by Professor Mellors when directing strangers to his English department. The historians had never been able to think of a suitably crushing response.

Facing the entrance doors to the building was the Arts lecture theatre. Up a staircase (there was no lift) were the offices of the other subjects in the Faculty – French, German, Italian, Classics, Philosophy. Along the corridors on both sides of the ground floor were the History and English staff. Both subjects had one senior lecturer, two lecturers and one assistant lecturer.

The English and History Professors' own rooms lay immediately beyond their departmental offices, with internal doors connecting to the offices. Their departmental secretaries – strong-minded women who knew their own importance and brooked no nonsense from students or junior lecturers – thus enjoyed private access to their heads of department, and vice versa. The History departmental secretary was Loretta Poulson. Tall with brownish hair and a firm expression, her soft blue eyes were gentler than her expression, perhaps hinting at something softer underneath. She was in her mid-thirties, unmarried and apparently a settled spinster. But she was not destined to remain so; and this was to bring complications both for her and for the History department – as we shall see.

Professor Grey was married, but without children. His wife, Jennifer – small, slender, dark-haired – led a very quiet life. She was not herself a graduate, and she was seen at only a minimum of university social events. The Greys did, however, undertake some entertaining at home, which it would have been difficult for the head of department to avoid entirely.

Jennifer Grey knew vaguely that History and English were

in competition for status and resources, but she did not know much about the details, still less about the subtleties. This was her husband's fault more than hers, for he rarely spoke at home about his struggles on campus. Just occasionally she would ask a question about the Professor of English, whom she knew was supposed to be their enemy.

'What's wrong with him?' she once asked. 'He seems polite enough when I meet him.'

'Oh, he's polite on the surface, but he's always plotting.'

Unfortunately, Grey never explained any of these 'plots' to his wife. Instead, he simply assumed that she was not likely to understand. From her side, she was left feeling neglected and bored. Their sex life was perfunctory. At home, he spent most of his time engaged upon historical research. He had already published two major books. He had no hobbies.

Grey was much more responsive when among his colleagues at the university. Like his wife, he was slight in physique – of medium height, with faded fair hair, deep blue eyes and a purposeful expression. This could turn into an engaging smile when he chose. And he could be amusing in company. His whole demeanour at work – his stance, his accentless tenor voice – suggested energy.

His History colleagues were a mixed bunch. The senior lecturer, Adam Thwaite, was twenty years older than his Professor, having been appointed to the college as a lecturer before the war. He was mild-mannered and loyal; but on things which he thought important he held firm opinions. This made him a useful foil to his Professor, not too deferential.

The other three History lecturers had all been appointed by Andrew Grey. This ought to have ensured their loyalty. But one of them, Peter Price, a gaunt medievalist in his mid-thirties, had never settled. He was already looking to move elsewhere. Yet he had published only a couple of articles, and he was still working on his first book, which he was claiming as a masterpiece in the making. The next lecturer, Richard Corke, aged thirty, was the best teacher among the historians – a rousing lecturer and a tutor who could relate easily to each of his pupils. He was plump, red-faced, red-haired, and popular. He seemed likely to stay at Blackchester for the whole of his career.

Finally, there was Tanya Jenkins, the assistant lecturer, aged twenty-three, an Oxford graduate, only just appointed on a three-year tenure. Small, pale, brown-eyed and auburn-haired, with scarcely noticeable breasts, bespectacled, visibly intelligent – superficially she looked like a typical female academic. And yet beneath this ordinary exterior was there something more distinctive? Something which those who came to know her might hope to discover. She came from suburban Manchester; but – like her contemporary Joan Bakewell, who hailed from just a few miles away – when she went to university she had adopted what Bakewell would later refer to as 'a hybrid accent that no one could identify'. She sometimes took off her heavy glasses and peered short-sightedly into her bathroom mirror. Not bad after all, she decided – playful behind the glasses, almost elfin. It was a pity for her that contact lenses had not yet become common in 1953. Even so, what games might she find herself playing?

(3)

The History board met a week before the start of the academic year, 1953-4. There was the usual discussion about teaching arrangements. But not all was routine. Andrew Grey held back until the end to report what he called 'another piece of cheek by English'.

Around the table, ears pricked up. There had been, Grey announced, an attempt by the other subjects in the Faculty to reduce the number of hours History could use the Arts lecture theatre. Grey had been approached not by a fellow head of department but by the Faculty's assistant Registrar, Bob Finch, who compiled the timetable. Grey had flatly refused to negotiate: 'We need those hours. French has far fewer students. It's a waste of space for them to have ten students in a lecture theatre which can seat two hundred. They're lucky to be allowed any use of the place at all.'

His colleagues agreed unhesitatingly. Adam Thwaite, the senior lecturer, framed two pointed questions with his customary restraint.

'Did Daniel Mellors support this? Is it really English that wants to be given more lecture time?'

'Oh, yes. We can assume that,' replied Grey with a sweep of the hand. 'They want to hog more prime time. They would like it to become the English lecture theatre.'

He then took the opportunity to range more widely.

'I have blocked them this time, but one day we must have our own History lecture theatre. I intend, now that we've got university status, to press at Senate for the immediate drawing up of a new building programme. To include a big new Arts building – perhaps a tower – with History having several floors.'

There were smiles all round. All the historians were *with* their Professor in his ambition; but they were also smiling *at* him for his characteristic opportunism – seeking a way to benefit the History department while also advancing the interests of the university. It was typical of the man. He rarely missed a trick. But then the same could be said of his rival, the Professor of English.

Of course, Andrew Grey knew that as far as new building went he was pushing at an open door. More central facilities were obviously going to be needed if the university was to grow, and the Vice Chancellor had already begun to enquire what support for new construction would be offered to Blackchester by the University Grants Committee. There would certainly have to be a bigger cake; but how large a slice could History hope to secure?

Roger Walker was Blackchester's new Vice Chancellor. He had been appointed only six months earlier – not long after it had become known that the university college was to become independent. He was of course keen to make his name in the process of making Blackchester's. He did not interfere unnecessarily, but his steadiness in adversity was to prove vital. Andrew Grey had ensured that History kept its allotted hours of lecture theatre usage, at least for the present. But Daniel Mellors, the English Professor, never gave up. Backstairs pressure having failed, he now intended to take his demand to the Faculty Board. Curiously enough, in appearance and in voice Mellors was not unlike his History counterpart. A shade taller, perhaps, but similarly slight of build, and fair-haired and blue-eyed. Unlike Grey, he had a moustache, narrow and close-trimmed. Maybe his smile was not so ready as Grey's, but his manner was equally energetic. Being a bachelor, he had plenty of time to be busy. There was a touch of ruthlessness about Mellors, which Grey shared but concealed better.

English was already recruiting forty honours students per year compared with History's thirty. The difference was made up because History taught more two-subject honours people, such as History/Politics. If English could permanently outdistance History in student numbers, Mellors would be able to hint that he was doing more than the historians in promoting the national reputation of the new university, and he would be able to demand more resources accordingly – more staff than History, and first pick of new departmental accommodation when that became available. In conversations around the senior common room Mellors and his colleagues began to spread the message about their expanding numbers.

A frequent presence in the common room was Dr Tom

Tongue. He was the thirty-nine-year-old senior lecturer in English, appointed just after the war. He was a slightly overweight bachelor, with dark heavy features but with an engaging smile, much-used as he leant forward in conversation. He seemed always to wear the same old brown suit, which knowingly or otherwise matched his brown eyes and hair. Women found him attractive, and there had been various liaisons down the years with female lecturers or secretaries. He had made no effort to keep these private. But he had apparently kept clear of affairs with students, although some of his colleagues found this hard to believe.

He was an active Marxist writer and campaigner, better known outside Blackchester than his Professor or anyone else on campus. His name appeared regularly in the left-wing press, and often enough in the national newspapers, especially when he had made a contentious speech or been prominent on some picketline. But he was clever, for he always stayed just within the law in what he said or did.

This same sharpness was of course available to advance the cause of English within the corridors of Blackchester. Whereas Adam Thwaite was a quiet support for his History Professor, Tom Tongue was a fluent foil to Daniel Mellors. 'Tom' was known to everyone. At lunchtime or teatime in the SCR he was likely to be in conversation with one or more colleagues from any subject, talking about everything but very often recurring to the future of the university. And in such conversations he always assumed that English would be accepted as the central Arts subject. He rarely mentioned History, but the implication was that it was an also-ran.

Daniel Mellors regarded Tom Tongue with mixed feelings. Tom was a good teacher and organiser, but the Professor's ego was slightly bruised by his colleague's higher outside profile. Also, Mellors was a practising Methodist at a church in town, and so did not like Tom's wayward private life. They were allies rather than friends.

(4)

The Arts Faculty Board met in the second week of term. Professors Grey and Mellors were members ex-officio; Tom Tongue and Adam Thwaite were elected members. There were twelve members in all: the seven Professors plus five others elected by the non-Professorial staff. The Professors therefore had a built-in majority, if they chose to use it. The Dean of the Faculty was chairman. This was the Professor of Classics, Guy Johnson. He was a Virgil scholar of international reputation, appointed before the war, who could have moved on to a major university. But he had been born and educated locally, and after a few years as a fellow of an Oxford college, he had come back to his home town and stayed. His wife was also locally-born. He was now aged fifty-five, and seemed likely to continue at Blackchester for the rest of his career. In appearance and manner he looked the professor – bespectacled, tallish, stooping, with thinning grey hair, intelligent-looking, with enquiring hazel eyes, gentle in voice and manner, but quickly firm when necessary. He was a good Dean.

Guy Johnson had a certain presence when dealing with students and also with his colleagues. He welcomed the energy shown by the Professors of History and English, but he had their measure. He was content to let them pursue their ambitions, so long as they recognised him as the Faculty umpire with the last word. He could do this the more readily because he was known to have no expectation of improving the position of his own subject within the Faculty, which was dying in the schools.

Andrew Grey always humoured the Dean, even if sometimes with gentle teasing: ‘Guy, we both of us know you’re the right man to lead the Faculty. Why? Because, since you don’t have many students, you do have the time; while the rest of us don’t have the time because we do have the students.' Everyone understood that the Classics intake would never reach even ten young people per year. This meant that Guy Johnson shared his teaching with just one lecturer.

Daniel Mellors seemed to be less respectful of the Dean's alert detachment than his History rival. Mellors did not humour the Dean as Grey did. And one day such an omission might matter.

But in the meantime Mellors had gained an advantage. In the previous year he had given a series of late-evening talks on television, straight to camera. His subject had been 'English novelists from Austen to Hardy'. Television still meant only the BBC, and these talks had been in the self-improving Reith tradition. Mellors had come over at his most lively, even provocative. He had praised Jane Austen for her concise observation: 'unlike wordy Trollope, her novels are not too long'. And he had challengingly dismissed Hardy's Wessex as unreal: 'an artificial literary creation, not a breathing place on the ground, even though he lived there'.

Mellors's listeners had of course included many English teachers at secondary schools, and enough of them had noticed that he was a Professor at Blackchester. They started to advise their pupils to apply there as a second choice, even if Oxbridge or London was their first preference. Since many pupils were inevitably disappointed in their first choices, the result was that the demand for places in the English department at Blackchester in the autumn of 1953 had boomed.

The subject of student numbers was discussed at the Faculty Board meeting. It arose naturally enough as part of a wider discussion about the place of the Faculty in the new University of Blackchester. The Dean had made this the main item on the agenda.

Mellors launched the opening salvo for English: 'Our student numbers this year have exploded. Forty. Of good quality.' He continued purposefully. 'I reckon that now we've become known as a full university, with our own degrees, we can expect still more. Our new courses for each year are very appealing. They look good in the prospectus. We could accept sixty next year, and still more in the future.'

Here was a prospect of dominance within the Faculty disguised as a matter for congratulation.

Tom Tongue interjected smugly in support: 'Our new first-year introductory course – "Shakespeare to Shaw: What to Read and Why" – has started very well. I teach it myself. They all have to take it.' Newly independent Blackchester could now devise as many such courses as it chose.

Characteristically, Professor Mellors did not stop at self-congratulation. He turned his offer into an implied threat to History:

'Of course, we can't do it all. What's the prospect for other subjects?'

The Dean answered for Classics: 'I wish I could be optimistic. We depend heavily upon the public schools. They still teach Latin, in part because it's needed for Oxbridge entrance. But even so, Greek has faded.'

The languages – French, German and Italian – thought that they might attract a few more students if Blackchester got good publicity as an expanding university; but not more than a dozen extra overall.

Philosophy had eight first-years this time, and thought that it had done well to recruit so many. Three were mature students. It could not promise to do much better in the future.

That left History. Andrew Grey had deliberately delayed speaking in answer to Mellors's leading question. He was trying to think of a safe form of words. But he could not find one. He was left with no choice but to respond without qualification: 'Yes. I think History will be able to go along with English. We too have new courses in mind. They'll attract the right numbers.'

Bold words. 'Right numbers' meant at least twenty additional students to start with if History was to hold its own, and still more later.

It was true that the historians were preparing new part-two courses. But so far no direct thought had been given to the question of how to increase the History first-year intake. The assumption had vaguely been that numbers would rise gradually year-by-year as the reputation of the university grew. But now Andrew Grey had promised to match the English surge almost immediately. How on earth would the historians do it?

As they came away from the meeting, Adam Thwaite began questioning his Professor. Careful as ever in his choice of words, Thwaite spoke as if Grey must have devised a plan. 'Andrew, how do you see us matching Mellors's surge? How do we respond to the impact of his TV series?'

Grey had no alternative but to be honest with his lieutenant. 'I don't know, Adam. But we'll have to sell ourselves somehow – here, there and everywhere – and bloody quickly!'

Round one to English.

(5)

Of course, Tanya Jenkins, History's assistant lecturer, was not a member of the Faculty Board. Nor was Dick Rogers, her counterpart in English. Given their similar ages and their shared lowly status, it was always likely that they would come together.

When Tanya first arrived at Blackchester, she had met Dick in the common room. He was a personable young man, both in appearance and manner – near enough to the ideal of 'tall, dark and handsome'. He spoke with an easy public-school accent. Tanya had no reason to be distant towards him. He had already been at Blackchester for a year, having come straight from Oxford, and so he had been able to help her find her way around, literally and otherwise. On her second afternoon, after a chance meeting in the refectory, he had shown her over the campus.

There were two halls of residence, at opposite ends of the campus, built in the thirties and respectively called Wells and Cavell. Most students had heard of H.G. Wells, but by 1953 few – even among the History students – knew about nurse Edith Cavell's execution during the First World War. Tanya had been given a staff flat in Wells, but Dick had refused the offer of a flat in Cavell, and had taken a place in town.

After a few more chance encounters, he had invited her to his flat for a meal. Tanya had got through a couple of boyfriends while a student at Oxford. She was still a virgin, but only just. She knew that to offer such an invitation as a first move was a bold step by Dick Rogers. He might have suggested simply going to a cinema in town. But he was able to justify his boldness by saying that he liked cooking and made a good spag bol.

So Tanya went to Dick's flat, which bore signs of having been hurriedly tidied up. The table was clear, as were two armchairs; but the tiled floor had not been swept for some time, and the two rugs were grubby, as were the red curtains. However, the sink and kitchen equipment were clean and in good order, which was a reflection of Dick's genuine interest in cooking.

The spag bol was as good as promised, full of flavour, not at all bland. Also, he had bought in some expensive fancy ice-cream as a dessert, which confirmed that he was keen to make the meal a success.

But did he want to impress her with more than his cooking?

They had drunk red wine with the meal, Tanya having just one glass. Afterwards, Dick offered a choice of beer or more wine. Tanya chose the wine, intending to stick to just one final glass. Instead, she drank several, and as a result became quite talkative.

He asked her about her first impressions of Blackchester.

'Oh, quite good,' she replied, 'most of the staff are friendly.'

The slight unsaid qualification referred to Peter Price, the medievalist, who had scarcely spoken to her.

'Richard Corke's very nice, and I'm lucky that he's the supervisor for my PhD.'

A condition of Tanya's appointment had been that she registered for a doctorate. Her thesis subject was 'Blackchester in the Civil War'.

Dick Rogers revealed in conversation his hopes for the future. His three-year appointment would expire in the summer of 1955, so he was beginning to look ahead. 'I hope they'll make me permanent. But they said when I was appointed that it was definitely just for three years – that they liked to have new blood each time. But now, with this talk by Daniel Mellors of expansion, I wonder if they would offer me a new lectureship, as well as finding someone fresh for the assistant lectureship.'

'Yes,' said Tanya, 'that sounds possible. Why not? But you need to know.'

'I haven't said anything yet to Daniel. But I must. If there's no hope here, I must start looking elsewhere. Take soundings back in Oxford. I don't want to be out of a job. And I certainly don't want to drift into schoolteaching.'

'What do you think of Professor Mellors?'

'Oh, he's impressive. Obviously going places.'

'I meant as a person, not just as a Professor.'

'Oh. He seems all right. He's a bachelor of course. I notice he seems to be easier with men than women.'

'Yes,' answered Tanya, 'I'd noticed that. Of course, I don't really know him. I've only spoken to him once in a group in the common room. I know Andrew Grey, my Professor, a bit better. They look rather alike. And they're obviously both very ambitious. Professor Grey has the knack when talking to you of seeming to find you of great interest. Of course, it's only a trick. Flattering though. Helps him to influence you. Professor Mellors gives the impression of seeming most interested in himself and his own ideas. But maybe he's simply being more honest.'

Dick Rogers had come to know talkative Tom Tongue, the senior lecturer in English, better than his Professor, although this did not mean that they were friends.

'Have you met Tom Tongue?' Dick asked Tanya.

'No, not yet. Though I've seen him in the common room.'

'He's sure to make himself known to you. Marxist of course. But he can talk about anything.'

'Right.'

'Just one thing. He has quite a reputation. He won't only be interested in you as a historian.'

Tanya smiled, just a shade uneasily.

'With an attractive woman like you, he's likely to try something on. Up to you, of course.'

'Thanks for the warning.'

Tanya had noticed not only the warning about Tom Tongue, but also the implication that Dick Rogers classed her as attractive.

They talked for over an hour after the meal, mostly about Blackchester but also about Oxford, where they had overlapped but without knowing one another. They had each gained firsts in successive years. Both had hesitated about moving to such a lowly place in the academic pecking order. They agreed that they had not chosen Blackchester for life; they expected to move on eventually.

Finally, Tanya got up from her armchair. They had not cleared the table after eating.

'Let me help you wash up. And then I must go.'

Dick made a dismissive gesture. 'Oh no. There's not much. It won't take long. I'm really quite domesticated.'

They both smiled at this last remark. Clearly, they were getting on well.

How well would be decided when Tanya went to the door. A generation later and there would have been no doubt that he would have been expected by both of them to at least peck her on the cheek.

'Thank you, Dick, for a lovely meal. And for filling me in some more about Blackchester. You must come to my place for a meal sometime. Though I'm not half so good a cook as you are.'

He opened the door as if to see her out. And then he seemed to have second thoughts about what to do.

'I ought to walk you back. Let me get my coat.'

She started to dissent, but not very strongly.

And so they walked through the town to her hall of residence. It took about ten minutes. Adding this final stage seemed to take their relationship to a new level. When they reached the entrance to her hall he took her gently but without hesitation and kissed her lingeringly on the lips.

'Good night, Tanya.'

She smiled, only a little surprised.

And so, from now onwards, not all was tension between History and English at Blackchester.

2

The Numbers Game

(1)

The autumn term ran on. Tanya invited Dick for a return meal within only a few days, which was of course a clear signal. The meal went well. And so did the canoodling afterwards on the sofa. During the rest of the term they were seen together at the cinema and elsewhere. Their colleagues in both History and English duly noticed their attachment. However, its depth remained uncertain, even to themselves. Their long-term thinking was concentrated upon their academic careers.

Meanwhile, would-be students for the next academic year had started to come for interview, especially to the English department.

'We are snowed under,' boasted Daniel Mellors. 'I don't know how much longer we can go on offering an interview to everyone who applies. We've even had to press young Dick Rogers into interviewing. I've asked the Dean for a new post – someone qualified to be one of our lecturers, but who will spend at least half his time as our admissions tutor. Perhaps someone with school-teaching experience, who will know the world from which our applicants are coming. That would help our interviewing.'

The Dean accepted that English was facing an emergency,

and a new lectureship was quickly advertised. The successful applicant was to start 'as soon as possible'. Mellors had decided that such an admission of urgency would be good publicity.

This was not his final demand. 'We will need another new post for next autumn,' he told the Dean, 'chiefly to help Tom Tongue with our first-year course, which everyone must take. Tom can't teach all the extra first-years himself. He has his other courses to think about.'

Again the Dean saw the point. But he decided that this further demand had better be discussed as part of overall staff planning for the future. He therefore called a meeting of Professors before the start of the winter term in the New Year, 1954. He could have held it before Christmas, but he deliberately delayed. He wanted to observe how History and English were squaring up. He was not inclined to let English grab all the new posts that were likely to be created in the next few years. He even said so to the Vice Chancellor, who agreed that the Arts Faculty must remain in some sort of balance.

This line of thinking was by implication good for History, but for the present the Dean chose not to explain himself to his Professors. He had no wish to upset Mellors – at least, not until there was no choice.

Grey and the historians were of course very concerned about the developing situation. They could not appear to be against progress, but they had always matched English in staff numbers. Now they would fall behind – unless they too could find good reasons for being given extra staff.

Grey pressed each of his colleagues for ideas. 'We can't afford to stand still, while bloody Mellors preens himself.' But no one could think of anything that would produce the sudden surge in applications that Mellors's broadcasts had achieved.

However, Adam Thwaite did have one good idea, likely to

attract more students in the medium term. Publicise history at Blackchester through the Historical Association. This was a national organization which brought teachers and others interested in history into friendly contact with university historians.

'If we became better known within the HA, that would attract more people from good schools.'

The Historical Association had branches which ran programmes of lectures in many cities and towns, and it organised national conferences and summer schools. Blackchester had its own branch, where Adam was a committee member and a leading light.

'We need to target the HA, Andrew. I mean at the national level. Use it as a springboard for publicising ourselves, and what we can offer. Get the schoolteachers to hear you.'

Grey, although an HA member, had played no active part in the local branch. But now a vacancy had occurred on the HA's national Council for a representative from the local area. Adam urged his Professor to stand. After a moment's consideration, Grey agreed to do so. By standing as the Blackchester branch candidate he was virtually certain to be elected.

So far so good. But Adam Thwaite suggested that Grey should not wait for his reputation to grow within the HA Council. He urged his Professor to make immediate contact with the HA's president, Professor Norton Medlicott.

Adam knew that Medlicott was likely to be sympathetic towards what the Blackchester historians were seeking. He had just become Professor of International History at the London School of Economics; but before that he had been Professor of History at the University College of the South-West in Exeter. He therefore well understood from personal experience the difficulties in the way of progress for his subject within a former university college.

Andrew Grey thought this an excellent idea, for he was

always ready to make himself known to top people. So he wrote straightaway to Medlicott, and they met at the LSE ten days later. Grey was totally frank about the challenge from English faced by History at Blackchester. Medlicott understood, and responded helpfully: 'You, Grey, will get known on our Council, once you're elected. But you need also to become known at branch level. That's where you can make contact with typical schoolteachers. And the best way to do that is for them to hear you lecture.'

Grey agreed. Medlicott then offered to mention Blackchester in a circular which he was about to send out to members. He promised to name 'Professor Andrew Grey of the new University of Blackchester' as keen to lecture to branches during 1954–5.

'If I describe you in that way, the teachers will be interested to hear you lecture, but also to hear about Blackchester's newness. We have sixty branches. I guess you might get twenty or more invitations. Could you stand that?'

'Oh, yes. I would make the time. I would be willing to go round giving one lecture per week from next September. That could add up to more than twenty. I would be grateful for the opportunity.'

When Grey told the Blackchester historians about this, they were of course well pleased. But they did not keep their satisfaction to themselves. Grey urged them to spread around in conversation with colleagues from other subjects, including English, that History at Blackchester was being backed by the Historical Association, a respected national body. The department would thereby secure good publicity not only for itself but also for the wider university throughout the country.

This was of course slightly exaggerating the support promised by the HA's President. But Andrew Grey justified the exaggeration to himself as hyperbole in a good cause. Indeed, he was prepared to go further. He also started a subtle smear campaign against English – although he did not call it that, even to himself.

'This English surge is all very well,' he suggested in conversation with everyone from the Vice Chancellor downwards, 'but will it last?' The memory of Daniel Mellors's BBC talks, he hinted, was bound to wear off. Television was evanescent. 'We must not build upon sand.'

In contrast, he explained how the new History campaign would ensure that the Blackchester historians earned a lasting reputation within the Historical Association. As well as Grey's own shock-attack during 1954–5, Blackchester's History lecturers would be willing to travel round the HA's branches year after year.

'We are building upon rock,' was Grey's summing up. 'We can look forward with confidence.'

(2)

When Daniel Mellors, the English Professor, first heard about this 'sand' and 'rock' comparison he exploded. 'Hot air,' he exclaimed to Tom Tongue. 'All speculation. Only *we* have the extra students. Typical of Grey to build castles in the air. I shall say so to the Dean.'

And when Mellors spotted three historians, including their Professor, drinking coffee in the common room, he only half-controlled his irritation. He called out across the room, 'More plotting? I thought you historians dealt in facts, not fantasy. We can put real students on the ground. You say you're building upon rock. Yes. What I hear strikes me as very "rocky" indeed.'

Here was a good enough quip. Andrew Grey was left with no choice but to respond with heavy cheerfulness.

'Glad you've found some extra students, Daniel. The university needs them in all subjects. Not just English. Of course, you'll have to maintain your increase and add to it. We've found a firm basis for our planned increase.'

These optimistic words about a firm basis summed up History's hopes neatly enough. But Mellors marched out cheerfully. He knew that he had recently contracted with the BBC to deliver a follow-up series of talks on 'Victorian Poets'. This would keep his name before the middlebrow public in general, and before the schoolteachers in particular.

All this made an uncertain background to the meeting of Professors called by Guy Johnson for early in the New Year to discuss future expansion. The Dean knew that he would have to be careful. Fortunately, chairmanship was something he was good at.

He wisely decided to prevent English and History from going head-to-head straightaway. First, he held forth about a discussion-paper he had circulated. This outlined the problems and opportunities faced by the Faculty during the next few years. Then, after speaking for nearly ten minutes, he cleverly directed the committee's attention not to staff numbers but to student accommodation.

'Leave aside the question of staff numbers for the moment. Before we take more students, we must be sure that there is room for them – either in new halls on campus or in digs in town.'

He persuaded his Professors to agree that he should explore further the accommodation question with the Vice Chancellor and the university planning committee. The Dean was himself a member. It was obvious enough that the planning committee would accept the need for more student accommodation; but the Arts Faculty wanted assurance that, if it expanded fast, it would be given as much of that extra accommodation as it needed. There would be very bad publicity for the Faculty if it ended up one autumn with more students than it could decently house.

'It would shatter our attraction. The newspapers would be on to it. Full of stories of exploited students said to be sleeping three in a bed!'

Only after half an hour did the Dean lead his Professors into discussion of the question of future staff numbers. And even then he held his English and History Professors at bay:

'The largest subjects in the Faculty are of course English and History. I assume that this will remain the case. But before Daniel and Andrew speak, I think it would be helpful to hear what the rest of you have to say. Not only about any claims you may have for your own subjects, but more objectively what you have to suggest about the expansion of staff numbers generally.'

The French, German, Italian and Philosophy Professors duly spoke up in turn. They had one point in common – that not all the extra lecturers should be given to English or History. They argued that such largesse would distort the intellectual balance of the Faculty.

This was reasonable enough in itself. It also meant that the Dean had rallied the other Professors to act as a brake upon the demands of English and History. And since English was likely to be especially demanding, this was a brake especially upon Daniel Mellors.

The Dean had also deliberately done something else. He had kept History alongside English in the race for more posts. Andrew Grey noticed this and was quietly grateful. He was also glad to let Daniel Mellors speak ahead of him, in the hope that his rival would overplay his hand by demanding too much too soon.

But the English Professor was well aware of the danger, and presented himself as a model of restraint.

'We cannot say at this stage just how many more lectureships we may need. Yesterday we appointed a good man as our new admissions tutor. He will come to us formally at Easter, but he has promised to help us informally straightaway. I've already told the Dean about our need for a second new lecturer in the autumn to help Tom Tongue teach the extra first-years recruited for next October. I take it that is agreeable.'

Mellors looked round the table as if stating the obvious. The Dean half-nodded. Grey knew that he must not dissent. A negative response by History would have looked like sour grapes, and would affect the favourable response that he was seeking for what he had to say.

'I think you will all have heard about the deal I've done with the Historical Association. A very reputable body. It will provide us with a sympathetic platform. We can sell ourselves through the HA to teachers all over the country.'

Grey outlined the structure and the work of the association, and described his friendly reception by its president.

'Professor Medlicott was himself at Exeter until recently. He understands better than most our hopes as a developing small university, and the importance of historical studies.'

The Professor of English looked as though he was about to interject at this point, but then checked himself and wisely said nothing.

When Grey had finished, the Dean came out in support of History, although in careful language:

'Yes, Andrew, you've done well. All to play for, of course. We'll not know for another year or more just how many fresh students your lecture-drive will attract. Your lectures will have to be especially stimulating.'

'Yes, Guy, I realise that.'

The Dean's skilful chairmanship had meant that both the Professors of English and History had spoken with much more restraint and brevity than had seemed likely. English had got its additional post for the autumn, but it had not been given any precise commitment beyond that. And by implication the way had been left open for History to seek new posts in due course.

At the Dean's suggestion, it was agreed to return to the

whole subject of staff numbers at some future date. Precisely when, he carefully did not say.

(3)

Andrew Grey started to think about what lectures to prepare for the Historical Association branches. They usually expected to be offered a choice of two or three titles. But Grey had a bright idea – he would devise one challenging lecture, in the hope that most branches would take it. If it became known that he was going round from Blackchester with a controversial historical revision, it would give him extra impact.

How to achieve this? He knew the answer. He would blow a hole in the reputation of one of British history's most respectable Prime Ministers – 'Mr Gladstone'. Gladstone was remembered as a sober high-Victorian, but in origin he was a product of the Regency, born in Liverpool in 1809. And Grey had been researching Gladstone's time there as a young man. He had discovered that the young politician had maintained some sort of connection with a humble 'Hammond' family in the town. But what sort of connection? At the 1841 census this family had been recorded as consisting of a widow, three older children and a boy, aged four. Parish registers showed that the father of the older children had died in 1834, and yet the baby had been born in 1836 and had been christened 'William Hammond'. At the same period regular monthly payments of two pounds had started to be made from Gladstone's bank account to the curate of the parish in which the Hammond family lived. The first payment entry had shown the name 'Hammond' attached in brackets.

No historian had thought it necessary to explore this Hammond connection until Andrew Grey did so. Perhaps researchers had assumed that it was a worthy payment by

Gladstone to some parish charity. Grey discovered that before her marriage Mrs Hammond had been a nursery maid in the Gladstone family. So William Gladstone must have known her. Had he 'known' her in another sense? Possibly. Alternatively (and perhaps more likely), she might have agreed to take as her own a baby that he had fathered elsewhere. However, the child had died in May 1841. Significantly, the payments stopped soon afterwards.

Professor Grey planned to offer his lecture to HA branches under the challenging title: 'Young Gladstone, the Sexual Hypocrite'. This threatened the received wisdom that Gladstone, an intense Christian, had been a virgin when he married in 1839.

Grey could have published an article about all this in a sober historical journal, discussing and defending his new evidence before going on to suggest how the episode altered the received view of Gladstone as a man and a statesman. Or Grey could have gone more public by publishing a middlebrow piece in *History Today*. But he decided to do neither until he had gone round the Historical Association branches. He planned to mention his restraint about publication at the end of each lecture, and so promote a sense of privilege among his hearers. He wanted them to think not only: 'good new stuff this – makes you think about Gladstone'. But also: 'Who is this Professor and where does he come from?'

Such was to be History's recruitment campaign. Would it work? Could English be challenged? Only time would tell. From the autumn of 1954, Blackchester's History Professor would set out upon his lectures, and his hope was that applications to study history at Blackchester would grow markedly during the following months, so that in October 1955 the size of his department's student intake would be rivalling that of English.

'Gladstone's temptation will be our salvation' was his

cheerful summing up to his History colleagues. In the event, most of the HA branches did select the Gladstone lecture. Sex in history usually appeals.

3

The Bite

(1)

Tom Tongue had spoken to Tanya in the common room several times during the autumn term. So he had come to know her casually, but he had not targeted her. However, during the Christmas vacation his latest amour with a secretary from the registry had foundered, and he was now on the lookout for someone new.

One Friday afternoon late in January Tanya was sitting after lunch in the common room glancing through the *Manchester Guardian.* She had been talking to a couple of scientists. They had eventually gone off to teach while she stayed behind to catch up with the newspaper. She did not take one at her flat. Tom Tongue had been talking to people at the other end of the room. Spotting her alone, he came over.

'Hello. Sorry to see you left on your own, Tanya. Left to read such a worthy but wobbly paper.' He sat down on the sofa beside her, while Tanya sprang to the defence of the *Guardian.*

'By "wobbly" I suppose you mean its balanced approach. Its suspicion of Marxist certainty.'

Tom pulled back, aware that his chat-up line had misfired.

'Oh, don't get me wrong. I like to read it myself. In fact, last year they published a long letter from me about nuclear disarmament. You obviously missed it.'

'Yes. I did.'

'I come from Rochdale, the home town of Wadsworth, its present editor. In fact, when he was a boy our two families lived on the same street. When I sent my letter, I put in a covering note recalling our Rochdale link, and he replied saying he remembered my grandfather.'

Tanya melted a little. 'Good. With such a link you will know C P Scott's famous aphorism.'

'Yes, I do: "Comment is free but facts are sacred." I've no quarrel with that. But we need to choose the facts that matter.'

'And to be sure about our facts.'

'Of course.'

Their verbal sparring had run dry. But Tom spotted a chance to build upon it.

'Talking of history and understanding, I see they're re-running *All Quiet on the Western Front* at the Regal next week. Care to go?'

Tanya jumped ever so slightly in her chair. She had of course been forewarned by Dick Rogers, but she was still surprised by the suddenness of his new interest in her.

'Oh, I don't think so. I've seen it a couple of times.'

A plausible put-off. In fact, she had not seen the film at all.

'Ah, well. Must go. So many students these days.'

Tanya wondered if he would try again. And he did, three days later, once more in the SCR.

'I'm giving a drinks party on Saturday evening. Care to come?'

This invitation was more difficult to dismiss, since it was not so personal. Even so, Tanya might have invented a prior commitment. She hesitated, but then said, 'Oh, thank you. That would be nice.'

'Good. My house is in town. Not far. Station Road. Here's my card.'

Thinking afterwards, she really did not know why she had chosen to abandon her initial hesitation.

There were upwards of forty people at the party – a handful of left-wing activists from the town, the rest from the university. These included professors and lecturers from most subjects, some with wives, as well as people from the registry – a measure of how Tom took care to know everyone.

However, the historians were conspicuous by their absence. When Tanya came to circulate, hoping to find a few familiar faces, she gradually realised that she was the only historian present. She now knew enough about Faculty politics to understand that this might be a consequence of the heightening tension between History and English. Had the other historians all declined invitations? Or had she alone been invited by Tom Tongue?

If the latter, this would confirm that he was now taking a particular interest in her.

When she had first arrived at his front door he had certainly been very attentive. He had taken her coat talkatively and introduced her jokingly to a couple of registry staff who happened to be nearby.

'In the registry they don't think of us as people, they think of us as statistics. I invite them here to show them that we're flesh-and-blood!'

Of course, his warmth of welcome could be explained as simply that of a good host.

After an hour or so, the first people started to leave. Tanya was quite sociable by nature, and had talked her way round the room comfortably enough, despite the absence of historians, talking especially about the future for the university. She had found one economist to be particularly congenial. But she had finally edged towards the door, and was about to seek her coat in the hall, when Tom spotted her and called out, 'Don't go just yet, Tanya. Wait, and I'll show you my *Guardian* letter.' He had evidently drunk enough of his own refreshments, for his speech was ever so slightly slurred.

Tanya was surprised by Tom's instruction, but acquiesced, although she was not much interested in his Marxist views on nuclear disarmament.

It was another half hour before all the other guests had gone. Tom then fished a cutting of his letter out of a folder.

'Here it is. Sit down and read it.'

Tanya sat on the sofa and carefully read the letter. Its content was much as she expected.

'It generated quite a response,' said Tom as he sat down beside her.

He waved clippings of half a dozen other letters. She quickly glanced through them. She had decided that she did not want to enter into a serious discussion. She felt tired, and feared that Tom would overwhelm her with practised Marxist logic.

She decided that the best way to avoid discussion was to divert attention to the personal letter from the *Guardian's* editor, talking about Rochdale, which was also in the folder. She hoped then to get away before too long.

'It reads as if he remembers your grandfather pretty well.'

'Yes. My grandfather was quite a character. He fathered at least two illegitimate children. I liked him.'

'You mean you liked him – full stop? Or you liked him because he fathered two illegitimate children?'

Tanya's lapse into jokiness was a mistake. It emboldened Tom Tongue to become personal:

'Oh, these things happen. We're not blocks of ice. Many women don't realise just how attractive they are. Attraction is more than just surface good looks.'

Tanya did not know what to answer. Her silence encouraged him.

'Take your own case. You're attractive because you project a look of intelligence – while not being off-putting, because you also look very feminine.'

They were almost face-to-face on the sofa.

'Perhaps you don't know this. Or perhaps you do.'

He leant forward and attempted to kiss her, extending his arms around her shoulders.

She flinched, and tried to pull back, but she could scarcely do so because he was holding her with increasing firmness.

'Let me go.'

'Do you really want me to?' He tried to kiss her again, pressing his mouth forward more firmly than the first time. Her response was decisive. She bit his lip sharply – and not once but twice. It started to bleed freely, and he lurched back. She shouted out angrily, 'You're a beast. Dick did warn me. I should never have come.'

She dashed into the hall, grabbed her coat and rushed out of the front door. She forgot that her handbag was still on a side-table in the hall.

(2)

Tanya hurried home in distress. It was late and she saw no one except the hall porter. She had to explain to him that she had left her bag behind at a party, and would he please use his pass key to let her into her flat. He thought to himself that she had not seemed to be the scatterbrained type. He also noticed how she did not look her usual composed self.

Tanya slept only fitfully that night, but by the Sunday morning she was able to think clearly enough, although she had a headache. She decided to tell Dick Rogers what had happened. She needed to relieve her tension by telling someone, and Dick was the obvious choice.

So she went to his flat in town about ten o'clock on the Sunday morning. He was only just up, and was surprised to see her. He could tell from her tense expression that something was wrong.

'Tanya! What is it? Come in.'

She told him rapidly and rather breathlessly – while still standing in her coat. Towards the end she explained how she would have been prepared to treat Tom's first move as a foolish, unpremeditated act; but how she felt that his persistence had made his second attempt into an assault.

'All this is just for you, Dick, I don't want you to say anything about it to anyone ... And I know you must not get involved, even if you wanted to – being in English.'

He was of course very sympathetic, finally making her sit down on the sofa and sitting beside her. He loosened her coat and stroked her hair, but wisely he did not seek to kiss her.

She knew that Dick was in a sensitive position. When the other day he had sounded out Professor Mellors about his long-term job prospects at Blackchester – as he had told Tanya he intended to do – Mellors had led him to think that there might be a lectureship for him 'in due time ... if we get our desserts and if we can stop History being rewarded for building castles in the air'.

Dick had been sorry to hear his own hopes being linked to the defeat of History. But there was nothing he could do about that.

And, as Tanya realised, there was also nothing he could now do about her own unpleasant experience. If Dick confronted Tom Tongue publicly, Dick would run the risk of seeming to be disloyal to the English department. And even if his reprimand to Tom were delivered in private, would Tom – number two in the department – ever want him to be offered a permanent post?

So Dick prudently remained silent, and Tanya intended to tell no one else. Nevertheless, the story still leaked out. There were two reasons for this – first, the need to recover Tanya's handbag; and second, the nature of Tom's injury.

When Tom appeared on campus on the Monday his damaged lip could not be concealed. It had bled on and off all night, and early on the Sunday morning he had driven himself to the accident department of the local hospital. The wound had been stitched and covered with a plaster. The plaster was quite small but it was inevitably very prominent. He was given antibiotics.

Tom stayed at home all day Sunday, but he had a lecture to give at 9 a.m. on the Monday morning. He found that the plaster affected his speaking, and he cut the lecture short. Students speculated freely about his injury, while his colleagues asked directly what had happened. Some of the students' colourful speculation came closer to the truth than they realised.

'Oh, I banged into the corner of a cupboard door which I'd foolishly left ajar,' was Tom's plausible explanation.

It might have worked if Tanya had not left her handbag behind on Tom's hall table. Distracted by Tanya's rejection and by his own injury, Tom had not noticed her bag, which was lying in a shadow at the back of the table.

There could be no question of Tanya retrieving the bag herself, for she wanted nothing more to do with Tom Tongue. But she assumed that he would contrive some way of returning it to her. She had other bags, but the loss of her flat key was a problem, for it meant that she had to leave her front door unlocked.

She had mentioned the loss of her bag when telling her story to Dick, and he had remarked that Tom would find some way of returning it. 'Maybe not in person,' added Dick, 'although be prepared. He might just try to talk his way out of it all face-to-face. If so, grab the bag and slam the door!'

But Sunday went by and nothing happened. No one came to the flat. As the hours passed, the bag question began to add an extra dimension to the tension which Tanya still felt.

Both she and Dick were busy teaching during the Monday morning, but they had agreed to meet for lunch in the refectory. They usually went Dutch, but this time Dick had to pay, because all of Tanya's money was in her missing bag.

'Damn the man. I need my money, and I need my key … What can I do?'

Dick offered to ask Tom for the bag at his house that evening, without saying anything else.

'No. You can't go. Even if you didn't intend to confront him, he wouldn't know that.'

'What then?'

'We'll have to bring in someone else – someone reliable.'

'Who then?'

'I have it – Richard Corke.'

Corke was of course Tanya's supervisor, and she liked him.

'Yes. He'd do well.'

'I'll go to him now. I'll have to tell him everything. In confidence. Otherwise he'll ask why I can't go myself.'

So Tanya went back to the History department and found Richard Corke marking essays in his office. She told him as calmly as she could all that had happened at Tom Tongue's party, and how it had resulted in her leaving her handbag behind.

Corke was of course shocked – for her, but also for the Faculty. Such things should not happen between colleagues, and especially not between a senior lecturer and a very junior young woman.

'I'm not entirely surprised. He's well known, but that doesn't mean that he's well liked. There have been stories about his philandering. Several wives and secretaries. Not students, so far as I know. Perhaps he's had the sense to avoid that. And no mention of assault before this. Maybe it's the first time his charm has failed him … Your reaction was of course quite right. You gave him a chance to pull back. And he didn't take it.'

Richard Corke said that he would go that evening to collect the bag, but would phone Tom Tongue's office immediately in case he had already brought it in. Corke could of course have easily walked across to the English department, but he thought it best to keep his enquiry as detached as possible.

'Tom. Richard Corke from History here. Tanya Jenkins tells me that she left her handbag after your party on Saturday. She's asked me to get it. Is it still there, or do you have it with you?'

There was a slight pause while Tom Tongue collected himself. He realised that Tanya must have told her fellow historian all about what had happened. Also, he was genuinely baffled about the bag, which he had still not noticed on his hall table.

'Bag? I've found no bag.'

'Well, Tanya tells me she left it behind. I won't go into details.'

Tom sensed the menace in this last remark. He became conciliatory.

'I'm about to go home. If it's still there I'll ring you straightaway. If it isn't there, I'll still ring you.'

Richard Corke waited with Tanya in his office until the call came.

'Yes, it's here. A small black bag. I won't open it, but I assume it's Tanya's. I'll bring it to your office at once.'

So Tom Tongue was taking trouble to be helpful. Very prudent. But Richard did not want him in the History department that afternoon, with Tanya there.

'No. Leave it with your departmental secretary. I'll collect it from her office.'

By three o'clock Tanya had her bag back.

(3)

That might have been an end of the whole unpleasant episode. Tom would have just about got away with it.

And Tanya would have tried to forget, although not to forgive.

Instead, it all leaked out.

Tom's visible injury kept the story warm. Despite the antibiotics, his wound swelled up, and when he hurried into the English departmental office with the bag on the Monday afternoon, he had to explain what he was doing through a thick lip. Several students happened to be in the office, and they heard him tell the secretary that the bag had been left behind at his Saturday party, that it belonged to Tanya Jenkins, and that it would be collected by Dr Corke.

It all sounded very odd. Why was Tom not giving the bag back to Tanya himself? She had recently been seen in the building. And why was Richard Corke involved? These intriguing questions began to circulate late on Monday and during Tuesday morning.

It now became easy for both staff and student gossips to link the damaged lip with the forgotten bag, and to wonder if the two were connected in some way through Tom's party. In particular, two staff gossips from the Social Science Faculty had themselves been at the party, and they began mentally to solve the puzzle when they recalled how they had heard Tom asking Tanya to stay behind.

At Tuesday lunchtime the same two men met by chance in the common room, and they soon agreed that they had independently put two and two together:

'Ho, ho,' they chuckled. 'He asked her to stay behind to study some letter … of course with the Victorians it used to be to admire their etchings!'

'Yes. And clearly, once he had her on her own, he must have made advances. Our Casanova. And she bit his lip!'

'Painful.'

'Then she dashed out in horror … not stopping to pick up her bag.'

'And she did not dare to go back for it herself.'

'Because she wants nothing more to do with him.'

'So she asks her supervisor for help.'

'And, horrified, he collects the bag on her behalf.'

'All is explained. QED.'

'A one-act melodrama at Blackchester!'

The two gossips looked immensely pleased with themselves. Of course, this was not the best possible use for their first-class brains. Nevertheless, during the afternoon their colourful explanation of Tom Tongue's injury began to be heard all round the campus, and its truth was accepted by most of the Blackchester staff and students.

The students praised Tanya's sharp reaction, while the staff in other faculties and within the registry and library felt even stronger. They emphasised that Tom was a senior figure, while Tanya was very junior. Even if sexual affairs on campus had to be accepted as likely, the feeling was that Tom should have been much more measured in his approach to a young woman whom he scarcely knew. It was assumed that his judgement had been affected by drink. His injury was deemed to have been well deserved.

Of course, the members of the History and English departments were bound to react the most intensely of all the academics. Among Tanya's fellow historians – Andrew Grey, Adam Thwaite, Peter Price and Richard Corke – the question arose whether they should view what had happened to her in more than personal terms.

Their thinking soon clarified as follows:

1) At the fateful party Tom Tongue had in effect been representing his department.
2) Tanya had been a guest at his party.
3) Tanya had been insulted.
4) Therefore, not just Tanya but the whole History department had been insulted.
5) So Tom Tongue must be reprimanded for what he had done.

By chance, Andrew Grey was the last historian to hear the bad news. He had been at home busy with his next book, and had not been on campus since Friday.

After collecting the bag for Tanya and giving it back to her, Richard Corke had let her go to her office, where she had students to see at four o'clock. He rightly concluded that this would give her something else to think about. Corke himself went soon afterwards for tea in the SCR, hoping to catch up on the *New Statesman*. However, a Physics acquaintance soon sat down beside him.

'Sorry to interrupt your political education, Richard. But what's this I hear about Tom Tongue and the historians? He of the plastered lip. I hear you're involved.'

At first Corke had tried to stall, but it soon became clear to him that the whole story was out. Not only was it already the talk of the Physics lab, it seemed to be spreading around the common room even as they spoke.

Corke hurried back to the History department, where Professor Grey had just come in. Corke told him the whole story, for Grey had still heard nothing.

'Poor Tanya. I must go and speak to her.'

'Yes. And presumably you'll discuss it with the Dean. Whether it has implications.'

'Yes. I'll contact him after I've talked to Tanya.'

Andrew Grey walked across the History corridor to Tanya's office. Getting her bag back had helped to calm her down, and she was talking earnestly to a student about an essay when Grey knocked on her door. She was not surprised to see him.

The student departed, and Grey launched straight in.

'Awful for you, Tanya. Richard Corke has just told me.'

Before contacting the Dean, he wanted to hear from her own lips exactly what had happened. He soon concluded that Corke had not exaggerated. The fact that there had been a second attempt was conclusive.

'I'll talk to the Dean as soon as I can. He may want to see you, but I guess you'd rather not repeat yourself more than you have to. Leave it to me.'

Andrew Grey rang the Dean's office in the registry, and was informed by his secretary that he had recently gone home. He lived in a large house just off campus. Grey rang there.

Johnson had been told the story an hour earlier by his own Classics lecturer, who had heard it in the common room. The Dean had resisted the temptation to phone his History and English Professors immediately, and went home as planned. His thinking was characteristically shrewd. The assault was clearly a serious matter in which he would have to intervene. But let them come to him. That would underline his role as umpire, with the final word.

Andrew Grey duly rang him about half-past four. Daniel Mellors, the English Professor, did the same about ten minutes later. Johnson offered a similar reply to both: 'Yes. I've heard something about it. Serious. The question for the Faculty is – just how serious? But we can't talk to any purpose over the phone. Come to my office tomorrow morning.'

But he told Grey to come at nine-thirty, Mellors not until ten. He wanted to learn the reaction of the historians, who presumably saw themselves as the injured party, before bringing in English, the department of the culprit. In other words, Johnson had already guessed that this incident, personal though it was for Tanya, would feed into the History-English rivalry in the background.

(4)

Grey called a brief informal meeting of his History colleagues for nine o'clock that Wednesday morning – minus Tanya. He wanted to discover whether he could present the Dean with a common History view about what should be done on her behalf. He found that he could. The four of them all accepted Tanya's version of events, and they all endorsed the five-point formulation already mentioned – that Tanya's personal distress was not the whole story, because through her the entire History department had been insulted.

Adam Thwaite, the senior lecturer, thought that the Vice Chancellor should take the lead in reprimanding Tom Tongue; but the others – although agreeing that the VC must be told – hoped that he would leave it to the Dean to deal with Tom. Formally, this would make the reprimand a shade less severe; and yet paradoxically – because Guy Johnson knew Tom Tongue well, while the Vice Chancellor knew him only slightly – Guy would be able to make it more penetrating.

At ten o'clock Professor Mellors came to the Dean's office ready to report the English reaction. Throughout Monday Tom Tongue had stuck to his explanation that his injury was an accident, and his English colleagues had seemed to accept this. After taking Tanya's bag to the office, Tom had gone home. On the Tuesday he deliberately kept clear of the campus, but this was only because he did not want to talk about his facial injury, not because he knew that the truth was coming out. The fact that his lip was still painful had forced him to cancel his tutorials and lectures for the rest of the week.

By teatime on Tuesday all his English colleagues, including Professor Mellors, had heard the colourful new gossip. Young Dick Rogers had kept out of the English department as far as possible and had avoided conversations; but Tanya phoned him to tell him what was happening. They of course knew that the new gossip was correct. However, the two English lecturers below Tom Tongue – Alan Wake and Mark Smith – were reluctant to believe it. They knew of course about Tom's reputation; but they were also aware that he had managed his previous amours without apparent complaint from the women involved.

Professor Mellors told the pair that he was seeing the Dean next morning. The three of them agreed that Mellors must hear Tom's version from his own lips beforehand. The Professor therefore rang Tom at home, and arranged to go round that evening.

No one had told Tom about the story now circulating – the true story. Mellors therefore had to spell it out. It sounded like an assault, at least at the second attempt. But at the end Mellors made it easy for Tom Tongue to claim otherwise:

'Is that really what happened, Tom?'

Mellors's word 'really' implied doubt. And Tom felt able to respond accordingly:

'No. Not at all. Rubbish. I had hoped not to have to go into details. I expected Tanya would prefer to say nothing. Of course I had to explain my injury. That's why I invented the cupboard-door story.'

Tom still did not know just how much Tanya had revealed, only – as Mellors had now told him – that gossip had surfaced. Hearing Mellors's account of the gossip, he knew of course that it was close to the truth, but he was not prepared to admit as much.

He had invented the cupboard-door explanation, and – now that it was discredited – he was quite prepared to lie again. He cleverly explained away his first lie:

'I didn't want to reveal that Tanya had been involved. The cupboard-door story was as much in her interests as mine.'

He still tried to play down the whole episode. This was made more difficult for him by the fact that physical contact had obviously taken place. So any explanation had to accept such contact as an awkward fact. But, claimed Tom, he had only been trying to offer 'an affectionate farewell kiss' to Tanya as she was leaving his house. To his surprise, she had grossly over-reacted by biting him.

'She'd stayed behind to talk about my *Guardian* letter. I

can't think what came over her. She's young, but not all that young. Nerves, I suppose.'

Professor Mellors did not press Tom Tongue any further, avoiding an interrogation. He did not question Tom's timing of the incident. And he offered only one slight almost frivolous criticism: 'You should not be so free with your kisses, Tom.'

Mellors added that he was seeing the Dean next morning, in company with Andrew Grey, Tanya's Professor. He left Tom's house in quite an optimistic humour, forgetting that he still had no idea what Tanya had told her Professor.

By the time of Mellors's arrival at the Dean's office, the Dean had heard the whole story in detail from Andrew Grey, along with the assertion that History regarded the assault on Tanya as an insult to the whole department. When Mellors arrived, the Dean made it clear that he wanted to find a solution with as little damage as possible.

'I don't like any of this. The Faculty's good name is suffering. But if you, Daniel, can agree with Andrew about what happened that would of course be very helpful. We could then quickly decide what to say or do.'

Alas, it soon became clear that History and English were not at all in agreement about what had happened to Tanya Jenkins. Mellors had yet to be told about History's strong reaction, and – unaware of how his words would be received – he started to recount Tom Tongue's 'farewell kiss' story.

'I spoke to Tom last night, and he explained what had happened. He tried to give her a farewell kiss as she was leaving, and she over-reacted. He doesn't know why – why she bit him. Maybe she was surprised. Even so –'

The Dean cut in:

'You say it was a kiss as she was leaving – and so entirely innocent. But, as I understand it from Andrew here, that is not the timing given by Tanya. She says it was while they were on the sofa looking through the *Guardian* letter and other correspondence. Isn't that her account, Andrew?'

'Yes, indeed. Tanya's said nothing to me about a farewell kiss. He made a double attempt to kiss her while they were talking on the sofa, and she regarded the second attempt as an assault and defended herself by biting his lip. That's what happened. This sounds like an effort by Tom Tongue to explain away his misbehaviour. Compounding the offence.'

The Professor of English bristled. But before he could speak in anger the Dean had cut in, keen to avert an immediate clash between History and English.

'Oh dear. We now seem to have a conflict of evidence. About exactly when the incident occurred. And I feel the "when" may well relate in some way to the "what". I think we'd better not get into that just yet. I had hoped that we could settle everything immediately. But I now realise that I must see the principals myself.'

Guy Johnson made it clear that he wanted no more discussion between them for the present:

'We three had better hold back while I put Tom's version to Tanya. I'll ask her to see me as soon as possible. And after that, I will ask Tom to come in. Then I suggest we three reconvene – when I'm fully briefed. Please say nothing to either Tom or Tanya. Would five o'clock this afternoon be convenient?'

The Dean had taken firm charge, but the pot had started to boil. And he knew that it might soon boil over.

(5)

Tanya had seen Dick Rogers in her flat on the Monday and Tuesday evenings. They had of course spoken again at length about Tom Tongue, but not to any particular purpose, for Tanya knew that, while others talked and campus chatter had uncovered the truth, she was on the sidelines. She was glad to be there. But when the Dean phoned her on the Wednesday morning, she knew that she was once more in the frame.

She arranged to see the Dean at one-thirty. Before that, she hurriedly settled to have lunch with Richard Corke, to decide what she should say and how she should say it. His advice was simple:

'Say it as it was, Tanya. The Dean will have heard what you told Andrew. Simply confirm that.'

'Yes. That sounds right. Though I won't like having to go over it all again.'

'The Dean may ask you what you want to do about it,' warned Richard. 'Whether you want Tom Tongue punished. I suggest you duck that one. Say that it's a question for the department, and especially for your Professor.'

'Yes. I'm glad to duck it. And if punishment for Tom would add to the History/English tension I really am too new here to know what I want.'

The Dean received her sympathetically.

'I expect you can guess why I've called you in, Tanya. I had hoped not to have to. Andrew Grey has told me what you told him about the Tom Tongue business, and I had hoped not to need more. But now I find that I do need to hear directly from yourself about what happened.'

So Tanya had to say her piece. She emphasised that if Tom had not tried to repeat the kiss she would not have bitten his lip and would not have regarded it as an assault, but simply as 'a case of silliness' on Tom's part.

'What were you both doing before this happened, Tanya?'

'I had just read the editor's letter.'

'You were not on the point of leaving?'

'Oh, no. We were still on the sofa in the sitting room.'

The Dean had decided not to reveal to Tanya that Tom Tongue was claiming that it was all about a farewell kiss – nothing more passionate. The Dean had yet to hear this claim from Tom himself, and it was just possible that Daniel Mellors had misreported him in some way. And in any case, in delicate negotiations – and that was what these exchanges had become – the Dean liked to keep his cards close to his chest.

Tom Tongue came at three o'clock. Unlike his manner with Tanya, the Dean was brisk rather than sympathetic, putting Tom under pressure straightaway.

'Tom, there seems to be a clash of evidence about this unpleasant business.' The Dean used the word 'unpleasant' deliberately, making it more difficult for Tom to claim that it was all much ado about nothing. 'That is why I've called you in to tell me in your own words what happened.'

Tom, who was no fool, duly sensed that the Dean, although superficially still neutral, was signalling that he might become less so.

Yet there was little that Tom could do to adjust the direction of his explanation, which in essence suggested that Tanya had been foolish, rather than that he had acted improperly. So he told his 'farewell kiss' story.

The Dean responded by immediately going for the jugular:

'Where and when did the kiss take place?'

'Oh, in the hall, as she was leaving.'

'And it was not passionate?'

'No.'

'Are you sure that it was not passionate, and that it took place in the hall?'

'Yes. I can't think why she over-reacted.'

By now Tom was beginning to realise that the Dean knew that the episode had not taken place in the hall but on his sofa. However, he had been lured too far to go back.

The Dean could have blown up Tom's whole story. But he didn't, because he wanted if possible to maintain peace between History and English. With that objective in mind, he had decided not to say to Tom that he was lying but to say it first to his Professor.

He wound up his meeting with Tom abruptly.

'Thank you, Tom. That's all for now. I'll be talking to Daniel Mellors.'

The Dean decided to call the Professor of English in on his own, before the arranged meeting with Andrew Grey, in the hope that he could persuade Mellors quietly to agree that Tom Tongue was lying. If Mellors accepted this, it might be possible to moderate any History reaction.

At half-past four Mellors bustled in. He tried to sound in control.

'I hope, Guy, we can now get this business settled. I don't suppose any of us wants it to drag on. I've not spoken to Tom. Did he say anything new?'

'No, he didn't say anything different from what you reported. He says it was a farewell kiss which she resented.'

Mellors cut in, seeing an opportunity to minimise the whole thing.

'So it was a bad mistake on his part, seeing that he does not know her at all well. But no worse than that.'

'Possibly, Daniel, if it had happened in the hall – the obvious place for a farewell kiss. But it didn't – not according to Tanya. And, as I said this morning, the "where it happened" relates to the "what happened". Firstly, Daniel, it happened on the sofa while they were looking at the letters. Not in the hall when she was leaving. It was not a mere farewell kiss.'

The Professor of English winced.

'And secondly, even so, she showed restraint. She only bit him when he made a second attempt. She says she was prepared to shrug off the first attempt as "silliness" on his part, but not the second.'

The Professor English tried to rally himself.

'This is what she told you, Guy?'

'Yes. I said this morning that there was a conflict of evidence.'

'And you believe Tanya rather than Tom?'

'I'm inclined to. Such a violent reaction to a mere farewell kiss in the hall is much less likely than in response to a second attempt on the sofa.'

Before Daniel Mellors could answer, the History Professor came in.

'Ah, Andrew, glad to see you. You come at the right moment. I've now seen Tom Tongue, and have just given Daniel my reaction to Tom's version of events – that it was just a farewell kiss that went wrong.'

'You know of course, Guy, that such an explanation is very different from Tanya's.'

'Yes, I do.'

'And you know that we historians believe Tanya. So which account do *you* believe?'

The Dean knew that he now had to take sides, but he still did so only by implication.

'I've just been telling Daniel that I find it more likely that Tanya would have reacted bitingly to an assault on the sofa than to a farewell kiss in the hall.'

The Professor of English had remained uncharacteristically silent for several minutes. Now he burst out in challenging mode:

'You do realise that you are both saying that Tom, a long-standing colleague, is a liar?'

'We already know he's a liar,' responded Grey quickly. 'That cupboard-door story was a lie.'

'Oh, that was done to protect Tanya. Tom had to explain his injury, but didn't want to mention her.'

'To protect Tanya! More likely he wanted to conceal his assault.'

The Dean was concerned at the rising temperature, but saw a chance to move everything decisively forwards:

'I've had a bright idea. Suppose we agree to disagree over the precise nature of the crime. Might we not still agree over the punishment?'

Both Professors looked surprised, even baffled. Round one to the Dean.

'It seems to me that Tom Tongue deserves a reprimand from myself as Dean. He has distressed a very junior female member of staff. You, Daniel, say he gave her only small cause for distress: you, Andrew, say on the other hand that he gave her great cause. But you both agree that Tanya ended up distressed. Will you leave it to me to speak to him?'

Both Professors had been suddenly put on the spot. Dare they reject the Dean's offer? The Professor of English spoke first. In his heart he knew that Tom Tongue might well have been lying. He had certainly lied once.

'I think I might go along with you, Guy. For the sake of the Faculty. A speedy reprimand would end the matter, thank goodness.'

Andrew Grey now felt exposed. If he persisted in demanding very strong redress based upon History's version of events, English would resist. There would be continuing tension. And, although the Dean had implicitly accepted History's version, he had now made it clear that he did not want to fight for it.

Grey hesitated, and there was a silence.

Then, fortunately, he saw a way out for History. He realised that he need not concede anything immediately. He could let Tanya do the conceding. If she yielded some ground it would involve no loss of face for History, because as the innocent party she was entitled to be generous if she so chose.

'We must not forget young Tanya in all this. After all, she's the victim. Let me find out what she thinks. It won't take long. If she's agreeable to your suggestion, Guy, so be it.'

Grey knew that Tanya would indeed be agreeable, if he prompted her accordingly.

The Dean's secretary phoned round and found that she was in her office. So Andrew Grey went straight there from the Dean's office. Tanya reacted as he had expected:

'I don't like being talked about. If the Dean can end it all – good. As long as I can have nothing more to do with Tom Tongue, that will satisfy me.'

(6)

The Dean arranged to see Tom Tongue next morning at nine o'clock. He told his secretary to say that it was an 'urgent meeting'. This would forewarn Tom, and it might also rattle him.

Guy Johnson plunged straight in, even while Tom Tongue was in the process of sitting down.

'I've now agreed a way forward in this Tanya Jenkins business. With your respective Professors. None of us have liked the gossip of the last few days. Bad for the Faculty. You triggered that gossip by what you did at your party.'

This last was indisputable. Tom swallowed and looked as if he was about to answer, but the Dean hurried on.

'We both know what happened. So we needn't go over the details.'

Tom Tongue knew that the Dean was dismissing his 'farewell kiss' story without saying so. He also knew that there would be no advantage for him in continuing to speak up for the story. Persistent truculence would only force the Dean to call him a liar to his face. Tom was down, and he sensed that it was better for him to stay down.

'I have to warn you, Tom, that if anything like this were ever to happen again I would not try to minimise it for the sake of the Faculty – as I have done this time. I would take it straight to the Vice Chancellor.'

'Yes.'

'As it is, I'll have to report our meeting to him. I think he'll agree to closure now. But not a second time.'

Tom Tongue was deflated, yet also thankful. Normally a man of many words, now he had very little to say.

'I understand. Thank you.'

So the History/English kissing crisis was over. Tom and Tanya's brief encounter had provided excitement on campus. And the Dean's masterly interview with Tom Tongue had been remarkably brief and yet very effective. A model of its kind. Tom Tongue left the office a chastened man.

The meeting had of course been private – a confidential discussion about embarrassing details. But did such a blanket of confidentiality extend to the very fact of the meeting, or to its outcome? The Dean suggested to the Professor of History that he should deliberately leak the news that Tom Tongue had been given a warning. The Dean wanted this to be known, aware that he had not actually promised secrecy to Tom. He also hoped that such knowledge would reduce the chatter about Tanya on campus, and allow her to settle down. After a widespread gasp of satisfaction at Tom's punishment, it did.

4

Academic Board Games

(1)

Tom Tongue's injury slowly healed. But for the rest of the term students who saw him on campus nudged one another and scrutinised his face. He had been well-liked by the students in English, but for a while there was some awkwardness towards him, especially among the girls, although perhaps not so enduring as their mothers would have liked.

While fascinated by Tom's self-made trouble, many students were also busy trying to sort out their own sex lives. At the end of his first term Michael Young, an English student, had failed to find a partner for the big end-of-term social event, the Christmas Liberal club dance. At the last minute, he had been let down by a girl in History, who had preferred an invitation from a second-year student. Second-years were a better catch.

This left Michael in a determined mood at the start of the winter term in January 1954. Despite the fact that at first he did not even know her name, he had decided to target a girl called Mary Parker. They were both in Wells, and during the previous term he had seen her coming and going. Mary was a first-year History student from Sheffield – small, dark, bright-looking. Michael knew that their paths would never cross during teaching, but his hope was that he would get an opportunity somewhere – probably in the Wells common room, or in the refectory.

His luck was in. On the second day of term he found himself behind her and a friend taking round trays for lunch in the refectory.

'Hello,' he said smiling. 'I think we're all from Wells. My name's Michael.'

The girls smiled easily enough, for they had seen him before.

'I'm Mary.'

'I'm Joan.'

Joan Peters had become Mary's best friend on campus. She was a pleasant girl from Hull with a ready smile, straight black-hair and frank brown eyes. A picture of good sense. She had no enemies.

'I've seen you both around,' said Michael carefully. 'I guess you do History.'

'Yes, we both do,' answered Mary.

After choosing their food and paying, the girls took their trays to a table, and it seemed natural enough for Michael to follow them there. He made a few safe remarks about the food.

'The food's not bad here.'

The girls agreed.

'They do a good chip. I like fish and chips.' Michael looked at his full plate with satisfaction.

The girls smiled at him indulgently.

Then, daringly, he ventured upon a development in the conversation.

'I see Wells are putting on their next dance a week on Saturday. My friend Andy and myself are available. Care to go?'

This was a doubly bold move. He had not even mentioned the dance to his fellow first-year student, Andy Locke. And how would the girls respond to so sudden an invitation from someone they scarcely knew? They might have partners already fixed.

But they hadn't. They looked at one another questioningly. They hadn't thought ahead to the dance, and they suddenly feared that they might end up as wallflowers. They had gone to the previous term's dances in a group of History-department girls, but it had shrunk during the term as some of the girls acquired boyfriends.

'Er, well, perhaps,' said Joan. She sensed that Michael was more interested in Mary, which meant that she would be landed with this Andy, who was not there.

'Where is your friend? Let's meet him some time.'

Michael sensed that he was making progress.

'Yes. Good idea. Let's meet up at the union bar tomorrow evening. Say, eight o'clock? Andy's great. From London. An English student like me. He's in Cavell.'

So they duly met up. The boys came in their best sports jackets, the girls in neat traditional skirts and blouses. Youth culture may have arrived on city streets, but university students were rather behindhand in matters of dress, partly because of academic poverty, perhaps also because they were still a separate minority elite. Contemporary 'teddy boys' did not read books.

Michael's friend, Andy, was a humorous extrovert who got on easily with people. In the previous term he had quickly found a girlfriend, and (unlike Michael) they had gone together to the Christmas ball. But the girl had fallen ill over the vacation and had not yet returned. So, as Michael knew, Andy was available; and he was well pleased by Michael's initiative.

'You've done well there, Mike, old boy,' he told his friend after the drink with the girls at the union bar. 'I take it you've claimed Mary. Fair enough. That leaves Joan. I like them plump. Something to get hold of!'

The conversation between the four had flowed easily enough, even though the two girls stuck to orange juice. The men drank cider, but their poverty ensured that they didn't drink too much. Although Joan had already realised that Andy was to be her partner, Mary still wanted to confirm that Michael was especially interested in her. How to achieve this?

It was done by each of them contriving to speak primarily to one another even while talking to the group. When they asked a question each looked at the other. Mary liked what she saw. She didn't hold it against Michael that he had targeted her in the refectory. On the contrary, she liked his purposefulness. He was clearly more mature than most of the first-year men. She said so afterwards to Joan:

'Michael seems all right. Seems to know what he wants, without being too pushy. What did you make of Andy?'

'He'll do for now. A bit sure of himself, but he could be good fun.'

'Yes. I know what you mean. Fun, but perhaps a bit dangerous.'

(2)

During the rest of the term both couples got to know one another. This did not mean that they jumped into bed together, for in 1954 Victorian values still acted as a brake. Also it was long before 'the pill'.

Michael played rugby as a forward for the university. He had begun in the second fifteen, but had soon been promoted to the first fifteen. He was strong and hefty without being overweight or slow – an ideal forward. After a few weeks he persuaded Mary to come and watch Blackchester's home matches. She had played hockey at her grammar school, and could be described as mildly 'sporty'. Even so, her willingness to stamp up and down the touchline on bleak winter afternoons reflected more than an interest in sport.

Just once, Joan and Andy came with her, but by half-time they had had enough.

'Glad to see we're winning,' said Andy. 'But Blackchester don't need us to catch cold for them.' And he took Joan off into town. Mary stayed.

Mary and Michael were on the same wavelength – except on politics. Her parents in Sheffield were staunchly Labour, and she had followed their lead. Sober Attlee, who had presided over the creation of the welfare state, was her man; not Winston Churchill, now in his last phase as Conservative leader. In contrast, Michael was conscious of what Churchill had done in 1940, although not enough to cause him to join the Conservative club.

Aneurin Bevan, Labour's firebrand orator, was coming to the Labour club, and Mary was determined to hear him. As a club member she was entitled to a ticket. Spare tickets were in very short supply, but Mary thought she could get Michael one. Did he want it? To Mary's surprise, he said not.

'I don't like him. A Welsh windbag. The real man is very different from his public message. A champagne socialist.'

Mary did not press him, although she did say to Joan that she thought Michael 'unthinking in some ways'.

Because they were in the same hall it was easy for them to see one another even though their rooms were well apart. Mary's room was on the north side, looking out towards the town, while Michael's on the south side had a more pleasant rural view. Mary made up for her grey urban outlook by prettifying her room with prints on the walls and a flowered pink bedcover. Both rooms had the same spartan furnishing – one narrow single-bed, one armchair, one minimal pinewood desk, one desk-chair, one small wall-mirror. The cream distempered walls were in need of repainting, and the dark-grey carpeting had become crushed underfoot. The red curtains at the single window had faded and lost their cheerfulness.

Michael did not attempt to improve upon any of this, apart from sticking a few reproduction railway posters on his walls, which at least covered the marks where previous tenants had done likewise. Their parents would have found it all much too basic and shabby; but at least it gave young people freedom from those same parents, which was of course an important part of the university experience.

Being in the same hall might have led Mary and Michael into an almost domestic relationship, but Mary was mature enough to prevent this happening. One dodge was to take herself off to the library and to write an essay there. She could also go to Joan's room. In contrast, because Andy was based in Cavell, he had less chance of encountering Joan casually.

After a few weeks, Michael and Andy exchanged impressions about their girlfriends.

'I like Mary,' said Michael, 'but does she like me the same? I hope so. Yet she seems somehow to keep me at a distance. Even if I don't mean that too literally!'

'No. I know what you mean, Mike. Joan has told me I'm dangerous. What does she mean? I've hardly touched her. At least, only gently.'

In other words, the two young men were starting to realise that the differences between the sexes were not only physical. They had much to learn while at university.

(3)

The Tom Tongue 'bite' business had naturally been followed by all four students with real interest. The gossip had eventually died down, but during the term most students in History and English became vaguely aware of a wider tension between their respective departments. Tom Tongue even referred to it tartly in one of his lectures to first-year English students:

'You people are lucky. If the History department has its way, your successors next year will be made to study a course of theirs. It will be called "More Shakespeare to Shaw", taking valuable time from preparation for English part two.'

Michael mentioned this outburst to his History girlfriend:

'Tom Tongue seemed very cross with your lot,' reported Michael. 'What's it all about?'

'Don't know,' answered Mary. 'I'll ask my tutor.' All the students had individual tutors to advise on personal as well as academic matters, and hers was Richard Corke, the most popular of the History lecturers.

Their paths happened to cross a few days later outside the departmental office. Mary said she 'had a question':

'It's not a tutorial matter. It's about History and English. Dr Tongue said in his lecture the other day that for next year History was trying to force a first-year course on to English. He sounded quite cross. What's it all about?'

Richard Corke was naturally surprised to hear that Tom Tongue had been airing his complaints to students. The historians, when told about it, all agreed that such grumbling was deplorable: 'typical, always restless, in season and out'.

'Don't worry, Mary. It won't affect your year. The History Board does have plans for something new next year. Still being discussed. We'll settle something.'

Corke was being diplomatic. There was of course a lot more to tell about recent Arts Faculty in-fighting, but it could not be revealed to a student.

Tom Tongue's injury slowly healed itself into a residual scar. For the rest of the term students who saw him on campus nudged one another and commented upon the healing process. After the week's interval caused by his injury, he had resumed teaching his first-year course, 'Shakespeare to Shaw: What to Read and Why'.

Tom was hard-pressed by the extra numbers recruited by English, and he said so not only to his English colleagues but also in the common room. This meant that Andrew Grey, the History Professor, soon heard about it. And in response he came up with a bright idea – doubly clever because while it was academically respectable, it also sought to restrict the demands of English.

Grey discussed his idea first with Adam Thwaite, his senior lecturer.

'I've been thinking about our first-year teaching, Adam, and I've had an idea for a new course. We need something fresh for our first-year historians, but suppose we made it compulsory not only for all our own students but also for all first-years in English.'

'A bold move, Andrew. To set up anything in company with English would be difficult politically. Even if what we offered was right for their students.'

'Yes. But if we matched our offering to their "Shakespeare to Shaw" course it would be hard for them to dismiss us out of hand. Every first-year in both subjects could be required to take not only their course but also a matching course from us – perhaps called "Shakespeare to Shaw: the Historical Background". The two courses would be complementary, two sides of the same coin.'

Adam Thwaite smiled. He was impressed by his Professor's ingenuity, although he responded with characteristic caution:

'Well, yes. At first sight it does seem an excellent idea in academic terms, but let me think about it. Meanwhile, I suggest you don't let English hear anything until we've prepared our case. I suspect they'll try to rubbish it. And you must get the Dean on side before they hear of it.'

'I agree, Adam. They'll not like the hidden benefit in it for us. If the number of their first-years gets far ahead of our History numbers, teaching this course would partially cancel out their advantage – cancel it out by us teaching their students. At the same time they'll be teaching our first-years as well as their own. So will they really complain if the numbers we send them are not so many as the number they send us?'

'A shrewd point, Andrew. Tempting them to acquiesce in any disparity without further complaint. Of course, they ought not to complain whatever numbers we send, large or small. They're getting two extra staff. The heavy pressure upon Tom Tongue is only for this year.'

A few days later the Professor of History went to sound out the reaction of the Dean. Guy Johnson's support would of course be vital to push such a major innovation through Faculty Board.

'Guy, I wanted a quiet word with you about a bright idea which may come to the Faculty from the historians. In confidence for the present.'

'Of course, Andrew. Care for a sherry?'

'Thank you.'

The Professor of History paused and sipped his sherry. Maybe there was more to this familiar ritual than a liking for sherry: undoubtedly, it checked over-eagerness.

'My present business is this. The university is of course keen to reinvent itself. One way to achieve this will be to offer innovative courses. If we publicise these in the prospectus they will attract more and better students. So the historians are thinking about suggesting a bold initiative.'

'Good. But not too bold, I hope.'

'No. It's eminently sensible. We want Faculty approval for a new first-year course. I imagine there will be no complaint about its content. It will be called "Shakespeare to Shaw: the Historical Background". All of us, apart from Peter Price, our medievalist, will contribute lectures. And all our first-years would be required to take it. But here is the bold bit. It could be shaped to complement English's "Shakespeare to Shaw: What to Read and Why". And once our course is available, why not make both courses compulsory for all first-years in both History and English? We would teach their students and they would teach ours.'

The Dean smiled, but was not taken in.

'Interesting. Yes, I can see the academic benefit of giving them all an early overview of both history and literature. We could sell that to the schools. And generous of you to offer to teach their increasing numbers. But I wonder what Daniel Mellors or Tom Tongue will make of it?'

'I don't know,' answered Grey. 'I haven't said anything to them. But the academic case is surely strong. I wanted to alert you. But please do not say anything to English just yet.'

'No. But as you're proposing to work in tandem with them you'll have to discuss it with them quite soon – the shape of your course, and certainly the proposal to make both courses compulsory for all students in both subjects. I wouldn't want the first discussion to be at Faculty Board. The more you can agree in advance the better.'

'Yes, Guy. I realise all that. I can only hope that Daniel Mellors will respond positively.'

Both men knew that this would be unlikely if the Professor of English decided that this was some sort of History counter-attack. Which of course it was.

Thus far, Andrew Grey had revealed himself only to Adam Thwaite among the historians; but he now called all of them together for a special meeting of the History board. He circulated a short introductory paper, which revealed his wish for a 'Shakespeare to Shaw' historical course. He took acceptance of his idea almost for granted, and hurried on to ask for ideas about course content. Then, arrestingly, he revealed that he wanted the course to be paired with the existing English 'Shakespeare to Shaw' course. 'Given that the two courses would be so obviously complementary, I suggest that *both* courses should be taken by all History and English first-years.'

There remained more that was left unwritten. Grey

deliberately put nothing in writing about the political advantage for History of his plan – about the relief from uncomfortable comparisons with English which would result from History absorbing some of the teaching of the increased number of English first-years.

In individual conversations between themselves the historians had welcomed this political advantage. They also agreed that an academically respectable course could be devised. It might be made to embrace in passing the growth of 'Britishness'. This would link up meaningfully with the notable Scottish and Irish writers included in the English department's course – Swift, Boswell, Burns, Scott, Wilde, Shaw.

A draft History course proposal was soon ready. Grey sent an early copy to the Dean, but with a request for continuing confidentiality 'until we have talked to English'. Grey decided that the best way to initiate such contact would be to meet one-to-one with Daniel Mellors, Professor to Professor. He decided to give no early warning of what he wanted to talk about, no prior sight of the History paper. He did not want to allow Mellors the opportunity to consult his colleagues.

Mellors was surprised to receive a brief note from his counterpart asking for a meeting 'to discuss some ideas'. They rarely met formally, except at Faculty Board, and their social contact was minimal. Even in the common room they tended to sit in different groups. Of course Mellors was bound to respond; but he remained guarded. Instead of phoning Grey he phoned the History secretary and agreed a mutually convenient time – four o'clock a few days later in his office.

When Grey came in, Mellors could not help looking quizzical.

'Welcome, Andrew. Mrs. Jones, our secretary, is bringing us some tea. I confess your note intrigued me. You mention "ideas". I'm all for ideas.'

The History Professor had decided to build up his case gradually, starting uncontroversially. So he began by talking about the need for the new university to offer innovative courses. He knew that Mellors was bound to agree, and he did so readily enough:

'Yes, Andrew. All subjects in the university must show initiative. We reported to Faculty Board how we wanted to put several attractive new part-two courses into the prospectus, ready for next year. And of course we've now introduced "Shakespeare to Shaw" for our first-years.'

'Yes. Interesting that you should mention "Shakespeare to Shaw". We like the sound of that. A good umbrella for an introductory course.'

Mellors smiled. But he was wondering where this was leading. It was not like the Professor of History to sing the praises of English. Where was the catch?

Grey continued: 'You'll be interested to hear that we're going to introduce our own "Shakespeare to Shaw" course – with the subtitle "A Historical Introduction".'

Mellors stiffened. He felt alerted, but was not yet quite sure why.

'You want to copy our "Shakespeare to Shaw" label? I agree it sounds crisp. But couldn't you think of some more political title, covering the same centuries?' He smiled mischievously. 'I know. How about "From Elizabeth One to Elizabeth Two"? That sounds lively. History up to the minute, ending with the recent coronation.'

Andrew Grey knew that he was in danger of losing momentum, for Mellors was almost laughing at him. So he responded in kind with a good piece of dismissive humour:

'Yes. We could then play "God save the Queen" after every lecture!'

Mellors laughed in spite of himself. Grey had regained the initiative.

'But we have used your label because we found it a good

way of relating your literary figures to our history. Shakespeare and the others are of course part of history as well as part of literature.'

Mellors was now certain that a challenge lurked somewhere, but he could not yet isolate it. So he decided to force his rival to come clean.

'Right then, Andrew. A good introductory course for your History students. But why are you asking me for an opinion? It would be nodded through at Faculty Board. I certainly wouldn't oppose it. I suppose we might grumble about you pinching our "Shakespeare to Shaw" label, but we wouldn't fight a war against it.'

Mellors was sure that copying a course title could not be the only reason why 'tricky' Andrew Grey had come to see him.

At this point Mrs Jones came in with the tea, prompting a slight relaxation in atmosphere. When they settled down again, Grey sensed that this was the best moment he was likely to get to bring forward his most sensitive proposal. He still chose his words carefully, and he tried adroitly to speak for the Faculty as much as for History:

'The two courses would of course be complementary, Daniel. And that being so, we historians have been wondering if the Faculty should build upon that. Why not make both courses compulsory for all History and English first-years? It would give them all an excellent basis for more specific work in part two.'

Mellors did not immediately suspect the student number calculations behind Grey's proposal. But he still tried to be dismissive, for he wanted no close dealings with Andrew Grey and his colleagues. He had never wanted closeness, and the Tom Tongue/Tanya Jenkins business had only added to his reluctance.

'Well, Andrew, we would have to think carefully about that. Very carefully. Our first-years would lose one of their literature courses. They have to choose two others, apart from "Shakespeare to Shaw". These prepare them for deeper study in part two. One is on 'Critical Method'. Why divert them to a History course?'

'Because historical breadth would feed their literary depth in part two. Shakespeare was an Elizabethan as well as a writer of plays.'

Mellors decided to wind the discussion up.

'Anything more, Andrew? Any other bold ideas? If not, leave me to talk about this with my colleagues. Tom Tongue in particular. I presume you'll be sending a paper to Faculty Board. If you let me have an early sight of that, we might be able to table a written response. Have you said anything to the Dean?'

'Yes. I gave him an outline. I said that I would be contacting you. He said that he would want us to come to the board with as much agreement as possible. Not start from scratch there.'

'Yes. But that assumes there is something for us to settle. English may not want anything to happen.'

The Professor of History now realised that he would gain nothing by prolonging the discussion – no point in provoking Mellors into more negatives.

'Well, Daniel. I'll leave it with you for the moment. Let me know what your colleagues think.'

After Grey had left the English department, Professor Mellors went straight to Tom Tongue's office, where Tom was preparing a lecture – appropriately enough, it was for 'Shakespeare to Shaw'.

'You'll never believe this, Tom. I still can't. I've just seen Andrew Grey. He arranged to visit me. He says the historians want to work with us. At least, they want to run a first-year course in parallel with yours – their own "Shakespeare to Shaw". And more serious, they want all our students and all theirs to take both courses. They say theirs would be an historical introduction which would match our literary introduction.'

Tom Tongue winced. 'Good grief. What brought this on? Amazing. It's plausible, I suppose. But what are they really up to? I suppose there's a case for saying that our people would benefit from some history. But why such concern for our students? It doesn't ring true.'

'No. There must be something in it for them. Why would they want to teach our growing number of students?' Professor Mellors's face suddenly lit up. 'That's it! Growing numbers. This would be a way for History to seem not to be falling so far behind – even if they can't keep up with us in recruiting more and more first-years.'

Tom Tongue smiled. 'The crafty devils.'

'I always said Andrew Grey was tricky, Tom.'

'You did. What do we do about it? Do we have to respond?'

Mellors frowned. 'It's tempting to try to ignore it. But Grey has said that it's going to Faculty Board. So we'll have to give an answer. He's going to send me their written proposal. We'll have to react to that. As soon as we get it, we must have a meeting of our board. We must plan our resistance.'

During the next few days Andrew Grey was busy writing up History's proposal. He composed a first draft with help from Adam Thwaite, and then called a History Board meeting for comment. Discussion of content and of teaching took up all of the meeting's time – how many lectures upon which subjects? Who would give each lecture? Professor Grey said that he would himself give the first lecture, which would be an overview of the course. To her surprise, Tanya Jenkins was allocated the next three lectures, ranging through the seventeenth century. She had expected that Richard Corke would take them. Nobody at the History meeting mentioned the political spin-off until Professor Grey did so at the end:

'We all know about the political relief for us implicit in this proposal. But I do not think we should discuss it here. That would give it formal recognition. I ask you not to speak about it to anyone outside – not even to the Dean. We must argue our case entirely on academic grounds. If we're charged at the board with ulterior motives, I will of course respond. But just what I say must depend upon how the discussion has gone.'

The historians all agreed with this line. The less said the better. Nonetheless, it was a curious state of affairs. Would they have proposed offering this course to English students simply on its merits? They preferred not to ask. Grey sent the finalised History proposal to the Dean and (as promised) to Professor Mellors. Mellors then called a meeting of the English board. He plunged straight in:

'We've all said in conversation that we don't like this History proposal. But now we have to say so formally, for transmission to Faculty Board. What line do we take? The course content is entirely reasonable. Outline history. We can't fault that. Fair enough, if they want their students to take it. But why ours? That's the key question.'

Tom Tongue answered. 'We all know the real reason. To undermine our lead in student numbers! We might have to say so – bluntly. It would be difficult to argue against on academic grounds. Yet to leave space for our first-years to take it, our students would have to do without an English course. Possible to complain about that, but it might sound a bit like whining.'

'Yes. It might,' responded Mark Smith. 'It would sound even worse if we opposed their course totally. We must make it clear that we accept their course in itself – for their own students.'

Alan Wake agreed. 'Definitely. We must not be wrong-footed. No course proposed by any subject board is ever likely to be rejected outright. The point of contention here is that History is proposing something not only for itself, but also for another board. We are under no obligation to accept.'

'I agree. Let's make an issue of this,' decided their Professor. 'Claim it as a threat to our academic integrity. I think I can get French to support us, and probably German and Italian. And meanwhile we can flatly refuse to go into detailed discussions with History about course content.'

There was unanimous agreement. But there was also a subtext, as Mellors explained:

'We must try to avoid saying anything about what we believe to be History's real motive. Not unless we have to. I mean History's double-dealing. Its concealed purpose.'

But Tom Tongue added a warning. 'It's not certain that we will get a majority for academic integrity. It sounds good at first hearing. A striking phrase. But it's a bit self-centred. People round the table may not want to sound selfish. If the debate seems to be running away from us, we'll have no choice but to drop our atom-bomb. Expose History's deviousness. If we do have to drop the bomb, the fall-out will be uncomfortable. We'll need allies. I think we should mention our suspicions to friendly board members ahead of the meeting.'

Mellors agreed. 'Yes. But let's express ourselves gently. Let's say "History may be up to something", but let's not speak too strongly. Be matter-of-fact. Not angry. And let's still give most emphasis in conversation to our concern for academic integrity. That's our starting point.'

This summing-up revealed Daniel Mellors at his most shrewd. He was sometimes 'bull-at-a-gate', but only when he chose to be.

Andrew Grey knew that the English board was meeting, and next morning he sent Mellors a note. It hoped that English had come to a 'positive conclusion', and said that if Mellors and his colleagues wanted to comment upon the content of the proposed course, 'We would be glad to get down to details. One way forward would be for Adam Thwaite to talk first to Tom Tongue.'

In response to his sweet reason, Grey was surprised to receive a rapid and dismissive reply. At worst, he had expected English to bury his proposal in difficulties. Instead, Mellors's language was brief and direct:

Dear Professor Grey,
Thank you for your note. The English board has considered History's 'Shakespeare to Shaw' proposal. We agreed unanimously that we did not want any teaching of our first-year students to be taken out of our hands. Academic integrity requires us to keep continuous control of all our teaching. I will copy this note to the Dean for circulation before the next Faculty Board meeting.
Yours sincerely,
Daniel Mellors

Grey immediately discussed this letter with Adam Thwaite. 'What now, Adam? Do we abandon the proposal to teach the English first-years, or do we stick to our guns at Faculty Board?'

'We're bound to press on. Our proposal is perfectly reasonable on academic grounds. To give up without further discussion would make us look weak. English would crow behind their hands.'

'Yes, Adam. My thinking entirely. We must prepare for battle at Faculty Board.'

Neither man spoke about what to do if English dropped its 'atom-bomb' by saying that History had an ulterior motive.

(4)

Faculty Board duly met in the middle of term. The Dean had placed History's proposal well down the agenda. He anticipated that there would be much talk and probably tension. So first he wanted to clear through as much other business as possible.

Both Grey and Mellors had tried to lobby him in advance of the meeting, but he had been deliberately non-committal:

'As Dean I'm neutral, committed only to what is best for the Faculty. As Professor of Classics I've not come to any conclusion. I want to hear what board members think. All I will say is that there are three issues. First: do we believe that the Faculty should accept the possibility of one board offering a course to part-one students from another board? Second: should any such course be compulsory for the other board's students? Third: if such a possibility is accepted by Faculty Board, is the proposed History course academically suitable?'

The Dean repeated these thoughts when he introduced the discussion at the board meeting. He then called upon Andrew Grey to make History's proposal. 'We're now a full university. We can stretch our wings. Indeed, we're expected to do so by the Grants Committee. They will give most support, financial or otherwise, to high-flyers. They've already said that for Blackchester they expect the Arts Faculty to lead the way. So let us be high-flyers. Let's promote lively new courses. All of us have already devised some specialist courses for part two next year. But in part one let's show breadth. Let's expose students to more than one discipline. Not just English courses for Eng. Lit. students, not just History courses for historians.

'In the detailed proposal before you, we're proposing to ask our English colleagues to teach our students, and we're offering to teach their students in return. This will stretch all our students academically. It will also look attractive in the prospectus. The schools will like it. And this may be only a first step. Other subjects in the Faculty may wish to broaden their part-one contributions in some similar way. The possibilities are many. An outline course in philosophy; an introductory course in German or Italian culture. And so on.' At this Grey briefly stopped and smiled. 'All taught in English of course! Students would have to be guided by their tutors to select a sensible spread. But such a stimulating breadth of choice would be good for us all.'

The eleven other members of the board were listening carefully, and were expecting more. Grey had intended to talk about the particular content of his proposed History course. But he knew that board members had already been given the details in writing in front of them. He realised that he could make more of an impact by suddenly stopping at this point, leaving fresh in the minds of his hearers the unexpected and important suggestion that new courses might be offered by other, smaller subjects. He wanted to exploit their self-interest. He was tempting them to begin to wonder if they too might be allowed to share in the teaching of the growing number of English or History first-years. This would give them more to do, and so would protect their futures. They might even one day aspire to extra posts. Having made the History proposal look like a precedent from which other subjects might benefit in the future, Grey hoped that they would be more likely to vote for his proposal in the present. This turned out to be a shrewd calculation.

The Dean called upon the Professor of English for his response. In doing so, did Guy Johnson's tone imply criticism of the brevity of Mellors's note to his History colleague? 'We have all read your brief note to Professor Grey, Daniel. You will obviously want to expand on that.'

Mellors was worried, for he realised that his rival had made a strong appeal for votes, the stronger for being an appeal to the self-interest of the smaller subjects. English had not anticipated this. Deviousness, he reminded himself, was 'tricky' Grey's speciality.

He still began as planned by emphasising the theme of academic integrity:

'The main thing that concerns English about this proposal is its challenge to our academic integrity. This History course is no doubt good in itself, good history, but it has not been shaped by us. Only we understand our incoming students and what we want from them in their first-year. After all, the first-year is not something in itself, something separate. It ought to be a preparation for the more sophisticated work which follows in part two, and leads to a degree. The same questioning must apply with regard to History's first-years. Why distract them? The History board wants us to teach their students our 'Shakespeare to Shaw' course. But we are not best qualified to teach History students, students who have decided not to study literature. I'm not saying our teaching would be disastrous. But would not History's first-years be better prepared for part two if they took courses devised by and taught by historians?'

Mellors continued in this vein for about five minutes. He was clear enough, but not quite as sharp as his History rival. The Dean then threw the discussion open and Dr Corke spoke in support of his Professor.

'Remember at A-level most of the kids do History *and* English; or English *and* History. Both. Probably with a language as well. Schools would look favourably on us for continuing that breadth.'

The Professor of Italian warmed to the idea of a course on Italian culture, as Grey had suggested by way of example:

'We could certainly teach it. How about "From Machiavelli to Mussolini"?' There was laughter all around the table. 'Glad you realise that was a joke. But we could offer something.'

The Professor of German was more sober, but equally interested. What about Classics? Guy Johnson decided to say nothing on behalf of his subject, not wanting to risk compromising his neutrality as Dean.

Daniel Mellors sensed that the discussion was drifting away

from English. He repeated his academic integrity line. His friend the Professor of French endorsed it: 'I wouldn't like to have to teach uninterested historians.'

'You wouldn't have to,' answered Grey. 'If they weren't interested in your course they wouldn't be required to take it. They could look elsewhere.'

Tom Tongue realised that this discussion about possible courses which might be offered by the smaller subjects was implying that History's proposal for a non-History course of some sort to be taken by all first-year historians was being taken for granted. However, the latest idea seemed to be that such a course need not necessarily be 'Shakespeare to Shaw' from English, but could come from another subject. In his search for allies Grey seemed to be increasingly ready to accept this possibility.

Mellors decided that English had no choice but to drop its 'atom-bomb'. 'We seem to be drifting into I know not what – blindfolded by the historians. I wonder how much History is really interested in broadening the horizons of our first-year students.'

'What do you mean?', asked the History Professor sharply, suddenly on the alert.

'I mean that we heard nothing about History offering courses to our students until we began to recruit far more first-years than History can manage. You are worried that we'll get more posts and resources in the future. So you suddenly offer to teach our students.'

'Rubbish.'

'You can't attract as many extra students as we can. So you're making work to protect your great-power status.'

This was a neat way of expressing Tom Tongue's charge. And Grey knew it. But he found an immediate answer, which was felt by many round the table to reduce the 'atom-bomb' from English into a damp squib:

'Nonsense. The present proposal does indeed relate solely

to History. Of course it does. We've submitted our particular course. But I've just suggested that all the other subjects in the Faculty should seek to exploit the same opportunity to teach cross-Faculty – with offerings of their own as alternatives to ours. We may be leading the way, but that's all. We could all pull together.'

English made no answer. And, noticing this seeming weakness, the Dean intervened:

'This is an important proposal which seems to be growing in significance as we speak. It involves History and English in the first instance, but in principle it has now been suggested that it could involve all subjects. Of course, there are obvious uncertainties, even contradictions. I therefore have my own suggestion to make – if History's present proposal is accepted as a starting point, we appoint a working party to explore the possibilities. Each subject to supply a member. No obligation in advance to go further. Merely to consider.'

Mellors spoke up sharply. He knew that he was being wrong-footed.

'This at least half-assumes that History's present proposal has been accepted. It hasn't.'

Maybe it hadn't, or maybe it had. The Dean had called the History course a 'starting point', but did that mean a fixed point? He did not say. Instead, he blandly hurried on without more contentious discussion.

'A working party could of course range widely. So let's proceed to a vote.' Votes were counted round the table, going predictably for and against among the History and English members. Grey had sought to remind the smaller subjects of what might be possible for them and he now secured the backing of the German and Italian Professors; but French had spoken up in support of English, while the eccentric Philosophy Professor also voted against. English and History each had two elected members, while the fifth elected member was a lecturer in French. So that made 6 against, 5 for – with one vote still to come from Guy Johnson at the head of the table. 'As Professor of Classics I shall vote in favour.' That meant 6 for and 6 against. There was a murmur of excitement. Mellors looked tense, Grey less so, for he had guessed what was coming.

'A tie, gentlemen. Which leaves me as Dean with a casting vote. A serious responsibility. Whichever way I vote some of my colleagues will be disappointed. I therefore propose to ignore that dimension entirely, and to be swayed only by academic and Faculty considerations. What would best serve our first-year students – students in any subject? In part two they specialise. Do they need to do so totally in part one? I believe not. We now have an opportunity to consider offering them some breadth in their work. The possibility has come about unexpectedly, growing out of a particular proposal by the historians. So be it. I shall give my casting vote for their proposal, in the hope that it will become part of a wider initiative. That will of course be considered by the working party.'

So the historians had apparently got what they wanted. The Dean had quietly directed the discussion in their favour, and he had cast two vital votes in their support. Mellors's failure to humour him in their personal contacts – and conversely Grey's readiness to do so – had no doubt played a part, even though the English Professor still did not realise it.

The Dean set up his working party. When Mellors complained that the board had not voted to do so, Johnson brushed aside his objection, saying that its creation had been implied in the vote which had silently accepted History's proposed new course. In any case, it was a working party, not a permanent committee.

(5)

During the next few days most members of the English board were feeling very bruised, Daniel Mellors and Tom Tongue in particular. Their objections had been swept aside by a majority of just one vote – and that a casting vote. Were they bound to acquiesce? Should they refuse to participate in the Dean's working party? Mellors called an emergency meeting of the English board.

'What shall we do?', asked Mellors of his colleagues. 'Go along with what has been forced upon us?' This sounded uncharacteristically restrained; but he already knew from one-to-one conversations what the answer would be.

'Not at all,' exclaimed Tom Tongue. 'We must fight back strongly. We could refuse to provide a representative on the working party. But if we did that, our misguided colleagues might well decide to accept the principle of cross-Faculty courses for all first-year students. History, Italian, German and Classics seem likely to vote for it. And in our absence, French and Philosophy would be unlikely to put up much of a fight. But if we had a representative present, we would only need to detach one vote from the other side. Perhaps German. We must try.'

They all seemed to agree, although young Dick Rogers said nothing. Unsurprisingly, Tom Tongue was chosen as the English representative.

'But what do we do about the "Shakespeare to Shaw" vote?' asked Mellors. 'That requires our active involvement from next autumn – teaching History's first-year students, and sending all ours to them. Fortunately, there is still time to stop that. And I think there might be a way. We could appeal to the VC to put it to Senate. Senate can of course overrule a Faculty decision, even if it has never done so. We would have to persuade the VC as chairman that we had a sufficient grievance.'

Tom Tongue responded:

'Yes. But we must take care to fight on our best ground. I've thought what that would be. There are two possible reasons for complaint to a higher level – unsatisfactory course content, or improper procedure. But the historians' course is sound enough in itself, so I wouldn't want to go that way. No. I would complain about the way the Dean used his casting vote. A casting vote should be employed to keep an issue open if at all possible, counting in effect neither wholly for nor wholly against. We could argue to the VC that our Dean should not have voted as he did, which let History through. Especially not when there was no immediate urgency and also a clear alternative.'

'Yes, the alternative is obvious enough now,' added Daniel Mellors. 'A pity we didn't say so at the meeting. I blame myself. But there was no obvious moment. History kept quiet, and the Dean played his cards close to his chest.'

Tom Tongue elaborated: 'The Dean himself introduced the idea of a working party to consider the principle of cross-Faculty courses. He should have left the History course for consideration as part of those wider discussions. Instead he voted the course through regardless. Maybe that was just about allowable. But his casting vote was divisive and unnecessary.'

'Yes, Tom. I think I could put all this to the VC. He would find it difficult to be dismissive, though he would not want a clash of any sort at Senate. I will explain how he could avoid trouble by insisting that our working party takes back History's proposal.'

Mellors saw Roger Walker, the Vice Chancellor, the next day. The growing rivalry between History and English was in danger of cancelling out the gains that Blackchester was making in terms of numbers. The VC did not want the University Grants Committee to hear about this rivalry. So he was glad to be told by Mellors that there might be a way of calming things down.

'You suggest, Mellors, that the working party could look at everything, including History's proposal – even though that has been accepted by your board. I would not want to intervene directly myself, but I could certainly talk to your Dean. You ought to have brought him with you.'

So Mellors left the meeting reprimanded but encouraged, and yet with nothing settled. It is a characteristic of Vice Chancellors often to be elusive, by accident or design, and Walker continued in this vein when he called the Dean in for a talk. 'Mellors seems to believe he has grounds for complaint, Guy, about your board's response to History's part-one proposal. Is he right? He's been to see me.'

'Has he? He didn't tell me. The proposal was accepted by the board.'

'On your casting vote?'

'Yes.'

'He thinks it ought not to have gone through on a casting vote. That it was misuse of such a vote, since there was no great urgency. He also tells me you've set up a working party to consider the wider introduction of courses like History's.'

'We have.'

'A good idea. Taking the temperature.'

'That's what I thought. We could see if the smaller subjects want to do likewise. But under no pressure to do so.'

'Why then, knowing the strength of feeling from English, did you press on with the vote when you could have handed the History hot potato to your working party for further consideration?'

'I wanted to concentrate attention upon the smaller subjects – leaving English and History aside for once. Their Professors expect too much attention. I had no idea that English would trouble you. Perhaps I ought to have realised. They're very self-centred.'

'Maybe, Guy. But they're the strongest subject not only in your Faculty but also in the university. And the UGC expects your Faculty to grow. We ought to humour Mellors, if we can.'

'You would like History's proposal to be brought back to the working party?'

'It seems reasonable in itself, and politically desirable. I don't want him to cause trouble at Senate. Trouble for you.'

Guy Johnson was not a man to fight an avoidable battle, especially as he still hoped to get what he wanted from his working party:

'Very well, Vice Chancellor. I take your point. I'll refer History's "Shakespeare to Shaw" proposal back to the working party, and get retrospective approval from Faculty Board for doing so.'

The working party met two days later. The Dean represented Classics, which meant that it had seven members, one for each subject. To match Tom Tongue from English, the historians sent Adam Thwaite, their temperate but firm-minded senior lecturer.

The Dean began by mentioning his meeting with the VC. He had decided not to say that this had been a consequence of a complaint to the VC by the Professor of English. Everyone knew about this, but Guy Johnson remained adroitly unwilling to take offence. Instead, his tone was matter-of-fact:

'You'll all have heard that I've talked to the VC about our part one. What we might or might not do to strengthen it. I've agreed to take back for further consideration History's "Shakespeare to Shaw" proposal. Not for comment on its merits as a course, but for discussion about the possibility of the Faculty making a variety of cross-subject courses compulsory in part one. That's why we're now meeting.'

The Dean had of course told the Professor of History about his conversation with the VC:

'No point any of us digging in too soon, Andrew. Airing our differences at Senate. The VC made it clear that, if we did, our Faculty would lose his goodwill. So I've had to tread carefully. But we can still be purposeful. If the working party comes up with a proposal for cross-subject courses in part one, and our board accepts the idea, it will be difficult for any

Arts subject to take its opposition to Senate. The Vice Chancellor would frown upon such persistence. I would be able to emphasise that they were in a minority: it would all sound like sour grapes.'

Andrew Grey nodded. He took the hint, and asked nothing more. The word 'English' was not even mentioned.

At the working party meeting, the Dean carefully steered the discussion through a series of loaded questions:

'Do we want to invite all Faculty subjects to offer part-one courses which will be available to students from other subjects? Should the proposed "Shakespeare to Shaw" History course be treated as one such course? Should all first-year students in any subject be required to opt for one course from outside their subject?'

Tom Tongue tried to argue the 'academic integrity' case, but he found that the three languages plus Classics were now clearly in favour of 'breadth', along with History.

Adam Thwaite, History's representative, had quietly noted that 'breadth' meant that English students would not necessarily have to take History's offering, because they would be free to choose a course from any other subject. But he silently calculated that most English students would still choose History's match to the English "Shakespeare to Shaw".

In addition, if all students from any subject had to take something from another subject, a useful number from the smaller subjects might well choose History's "Shakespeare to Shaw". This meant that History might attract even more first-year non-historians than it had expected from its original proposal aimed only at English students.

Perhaps the Dean had made the same calculation, although of course he never said so. 'I sense that a majority of us would like to take this further. I suggest that we ask our colleagues in each subject to come up with detailed proposals, except of course for History which already has

"Shakespeare to Shaw" on offer. I'm not sure about English, Tom. Is your "Shakespeare to Shaw" likely to be available to all; or will you devise something else?'

This last question was of course blandly assuming that English would have to abandon its 'academic integrity' negative.

'I really don't know, Guy. I can't commit us. We've not made contingency plans. We still feel strongly. I can't promise anything.'

A clear negative. But the Dean insisted upon being conciliatory. 'Well, fortunately, you have "Shakespeare to Shaw" in place. You wouldn't need to do anything more.'

That was of course true only if two words were added – 'not need to do anything more *but acquiesce.*'

(6)

The working party's report came to Faculty Board at its end-of-term meeting, just before Easter 1954. It recommended by a majority of five votes to two that all subjects should offer courses to part-one students other than their own – every student to choose one course from outside their specialism. Only French had supported English in its opposition.

At the first Faculty Board of the summer term, the Professors of English and French fought one last rearguard action in the name of 'academic integrity'. But because German, Italian and Philosophy had now changed sides, they were outvoted without the Dean needing to use his casting vote. This of course strengthened the case for change.

All subjects except English and French had devised new courses for offer to part-one students in other subjects. The Dean addressed this issue head-on:

'We must send our proposal to Senate for formal approval this term, so as to be ready for next October. We should include in the same paper the course details from each subject. I'm today tabling the details supplied to me by every board except English and French. I need to have their details very soon – for formal confirmation by this board and for inclusion in the paper to Senate.' The Dean then firmly grasped the English nettle, while at the same time blandly offering a way out:

'What is English going to do, Daniel? Of course, if you offer your existing "Shakespeare to Shaw" you need do nothing more.'

Mellors coloured, and answered with sharp brevity. 'You are holding a pistol to our heads, Guy – and you know it. I will call a special meeting of the English board. I can't promise anything more. You may not get the acquiescence you expect.'

The Dean was surprised by the strength of this warning. It forced him to realise that the contest was not yet over. On the surface he remained calm.

'Right. As soon as your board has come to a conclusion, let me know. Don't wait to report back to this board.'

The Dean had decided that if there must be an unavoidable clash with English, it would be better if this were in private and was personalised between Mellors and himself rather than aired in public. Better a joust in the tiltyard of his office than a battle on the open field.

The English board duly met. Mellors formally reported that its case for 'academic integrity' had been rejected, and that they had been told to offer a part-one course to students in other subjects – either "Shakespeare to Shaw" or something else.

'The first question now is: can we refuse? I get the impression from conversations with each of you that you are all shell-shocked, unsure what to do next.'

That was true, except that Mellors had not talked to Dick Rogers, his most junior colleague.

Tom Tongue spoke up: 'We have a right to appeal to Senate. The VC could not refuse us.'

'No, but the Dean says that the VC would make the Faculty pay,' warned Alan Wake. 'At the moment we're the largest subject in the Faculty favoured by the UGC. The VC could hold back our expansion. I've heard that Social Science is trying to curry favour.'

'That's probably just his bluff,' answered Tom Tongue. 'He doesn't want trouble. He wants to achieve this by persuading us not to press our case. But we could point out to him that there is an alternative. He would be equally satisfied if we persuaded the Dean not to press *his* case.'

'Maybe. But how could we sway the Dean?' asked Mark Smith.

'By remaining firm,' answered Tom Tongue. 'By saying that in no circumstances would we make an English course available.'

Here was the ultimate deterrent. Daniel Mellors underlined the seriousness of such a move, and in the process went historical.

'This would be civil war. Most other subjects would denounce us. Even French might surrender. Rather like they did in 1940! Would this be a "finest hour" for academic integrity? That's the question for us now. If we think so, we stand firm.'

Dick Rogers made a rare intervention. 'What would it mean in terms of procedure?'

Professor Mellors explained: 'If the Faculty proposal goes to Senate, we could insist upon opposing it there. In the last resort, the VC as chairman would have to allow us to speak. But while we would make it clear to our Dean that we would persist in this way, I could urge him to take it all back to Faculty Board for further consideration.'

Tom Tongue agreed. 'That's right. Be firm but give the Dean the chance to climb down. Even tell him in advance that room for a climb-down by the Faculty is what you are offering. Not any sort of climb-down by us.'

The Professor of English went to see the Dean next day.

'You asked me to report back to you, Guy, as quickly and clearly as possible. I'm glad to do so. The English board has not changed its mind. It still stands out for academic integrity, and would in the last resort insist upon explaining its attitude to Senate. It suggests, however, that you take the whole question back to Faculty Board for further consideration. That would give room for "flexibility" or "climb down". Some would want to call it the one, some the other.'

The Dean knew that he would have to agree. Otherwise, Mellors would use any refusal as part of his argument at Senate. The Dean of Arts would be unfavourably portrayed to other faculties as inflexible. But Guy Johnson also knew that he was being invited to oversee some sort of retreat at Faculty Board. Needing time to think further, he decided to be curt, and not to hear again the English case.

'Very well, Daniel. English was in a minority when we voted, but let the board hear once more what you have to say.' The Dean then added what proved to be an important gloss: 'You will have to explain not only why English does not want "breadth" in part one, but also why students in other subjects should not have it.'

The Dean called an emergency meeting of the Faculty Board for the next Saturday morning, with only the one item on the agenda. He had spoken in advance to each of his Professors apart from English. He sensed that they were growing impatient with the intransigence being shown by Daniel Mellors. Why, they asked, should their first-years be denied by English the opportunity to take one course from outside their specialism? Even Mellors's friend the Professor of French was now hesitating about taking the fight to Senate, when he heard the English case criticised in such terms. Andrew Grey, speaking for History, was of course dismissive:

'Their concern, Guy, for what they call "academic integrity" is bogus. They will always have it in part two. Some breadth in part one would be good for their students.'

The Faculty Board duly met. The Dean was hoping to detach the Professor of French from supporting any English complaint to Senate. If English did go to Senate, he wanted it to be seen as standing alone. He therefore decided to abandon diplomatic language and to explain himself forcefully.

'This would be washing our dirty linen in public. If English spoke out – presumably that would be you, Daniel – in order to proclaim its commitment to "academic integrity", I would be bound to reply as Dean. I would deliberately say little about such integrity in itself. I would simply point out that the board had reached a considered majority decision. It had weighed the integrity argument and had found it unpersuasive. Your persistence in forcing me to speak up for the majority would of course be tiresome for me as Dean. But more seriously, such a public rift would damage our standing with the other faculties in general and with the VC in particular. In the near future, he might well seek to divert to Social Science some of the resources for Faculty expansion which might otherwise have come to us. If so, English, as the largest subject in our Faculty, will suffer the most. You want more lectureships – you might not get them.'

Daniel Mellors bristled. 'Why would you not respond to our concern about academic integrity, Guy?'

'Because the Faculty has already done so. In requiring first-year students to take one course outside their specialism, how would this affect the academic integrity of their part-two work – their final-degree work?'

'It would dilute their preparation in part one for part two.'

'The displacement of one English course in part one would surely amount to very little by the end of part two?'

'They would lose the preparation provided by that part-one English course.'

'Yes. And have the benefit of breadth in return. If, for example, your students added History's "Shakespeare to Shaw" course to your English "Shakespeare to Shaw" would that not actually help their understanding of English literature in part two?'

There was a pause round the table before the Professor of French made a significant admission: 'A fair point.'

Uncharacteristically, Tom Tongue had said nothing so far. Was he having second thoughts? Not about the academic merits of the English stand, but about its political effects. He was, after all, an active Marxist.

'I'm worried about the VC. He's proving quite effective as chairman of Senate. He usually gets his way. And from what I now hear, I doubt if he'll allow any debate about our complaint. The Registrar seems to have been deliberately leaking this in conversations around the SCR – as a warning. The VC will hurry on to next business straight after hearing from Daniel and from you, Guy. No further discussion. We may not be allowed any opportunity to get the Faculty's proposal sent back.'

What Tom Tongue was not saying – but had obviously been thinking – was that he himself would not be given any chance to speak at Senate. Perhaps this was contributing to his second thoughts:

'We may have to settle simply for our dissent being recorded in the minutes. And yet if we can expect to do no better than that, I begin to wonder if it's all worth it. For if we persist at Senate in trying to reply to our own Dean it does now seem that the VC will hold our persistence against us – against the Faculty in the future and especially against English.'

Unexpected words. And Guy Johnson realised that he could treat this intervention as amounting to a climb-down by English, even though Tom Tongue had not withdrawn the 'academic integrity' argument. The Dean achieved this by taking Tom's words one step further. He now blandly pointed out – in the light of what Tom had just said about the English board's dissent being placed on record – that English had in fact already achieved this.

'That's very helpful, Tom. I'm sure you're right about the VC. He's been well disposed towards us since his appointment. We don't want to lose him. And of course English has already made the strength of its feeling known by the very fact of giving notice to Senate. That surely is enough. The notice could now be withdrawn without any inconsistency. If you do this quickly, the VC will feel relieved, perhaps even glad, and will have no reason to hold anything against us in the future.'

What could the Professor of English do but agree? He looked decidedly crumpled. Underneath, he felt critical of Tom Tongue. Dialectics were supposed to be Tom's forte. Yet where had he taken the English department? He had blown first hot and now cold – rather like the grand old Duke of York, who had led his men up the hill and then down again, all to no good purpose.

Be that as it may, the Dean had restored peace to the Faculty. And although no one said so at the Faculty Board, History had won its battle with English. One battle, but not the war.

(7)

By the long vacation of 1954 Andrew Grey had changed his mind about how best to publicise his new view of Gladstone – with its aim of attracting more History students to Blackchester. Instead of revealing his discoveries only to Historical Association audiences, flattering them by offering them an academic exclusive, he had now decided to cause as wide a stir as possible through the press. His chosen outlet was the *Manchester Guardian*.

This rising newspaper was read by Grey himself, and by a growing number of schoolteachers and university lecturers in places increasingly far from Manchester. Its editor, A.P. Wadsworth, was a historian as well as a journalist, the author of a major history of the cotton trade. He commissioned frequent thousand-word articles for the paper's centre page upon topics of wide historical interest like anniversaries or discoveries. These were written by rising historians such as A.J.P. Taylor, and were always kept suitably middlebrow, able to be read (as Wadsworth explained to Taylor) 'on the way to work'.

Grey saw his opportunity. He wrote to the editor offering him an article which made serious revelations about the young Gladstone. It duly appeared in August 1954, and it made the impact Grey had hoped for. Dozens of letters in response were sent to the editor; some of which were published, some not. Those from Gladstone's unqualified admirers of course expressed shock that their idol had been tarnished. 'He knew about sin,' they exclaimed, recalling his work saving prostitutes, 'but always campaigned against it. It is especially upsetting for him to be smeared in your great Liberal newspaper.'

Yet the more open-minded correspondents accepted that it was reasonable for 'Professor Grey from Blackchester' (as he was pleasingly becoming known) to enquire what the unmarried Gladstone had been doing during his twenties. He may have been a Victorian hero, but he had been brought up as a child of the Regency. And one correspondent made a shrewd point: 'Since no one ever accused him of fathering an illegitimate child, he was under no obligation to admit it, especially as the child died young. If a child had grown up, concealment would have been deception, but that never happened.'

All this of course provided Grey with the opportunity to write a long letter to the *Guardian* in reply to its many correspondents, published and unpublished. He was able to point out that several prime ministers had led questionable sex lives, including Lloyd George, the Liberal hero. 'Liberal party leaders are men, not saints, and all have been young men.'

So Grey's opening campaign had been a great success. It meant that the ground had been well prepared when he began his tour of Historical Association branches a few weeks later. His local audiences had been suitably primed: all wanted to know more.

Grey concluded his *Guardian* piece, and also his lectures, by making direct reference to Blackchester University and to the teaching of history there: 'We encourage our students to ask questions about the received reputations of figures in history, such as Gladstone.'

This was of course an effective point, scarcely open to question. Grey's final sentence offered a deliberately provocative swipe at his old university: 'Unlike Oxford, we're not tempted to indulge the reputations of old members, even if they are Gladstones from Christ Church. Such openness is one of the benefits of being a new university.'

All this good publicity bore increasing fruit for the History department at Blackchester. From the autumn of 1954 applications for the following year began to build up steadily. There could be little doubt that thousands of schoolmasters had read Grey's *Guardian* article and its related correspondence, and that hundreds had heard (or heard about) his HA lectures. History now anticipated recruiting as many as fifty first-years for the autumn of 1955, an increase of twenty in one intake. This matched the English total for 1954.

Quite a few of Blackchester's History students read Grey's *Guardian* article, even though it had appeared in the long vacation. And when they returned in the autumn all of them became aware of his publicity drive. Some were more interested than others, aware that they were academic pioneers.

'Do we care,' asked some of them, 'whether more people come here or not? Perhaps we do. But after all, our Professors are *paid* to sell their subjects. We're not.'

And predictably, the Professor of English remained critical:

'I'm glad History is trying to pull its weight at last. Fifty is an improvement. But will they ever catch up with us? Certainly not through articles about Gladstone with his trousers down. Anyway' – and Mellors paused before delivering what he regarded as crushing news – 'we now expect sixty for next autumn.'

Of course, the History Professor could not admit to any disappointment when he heard of this further growth. He had to appear to support all expansion of the university wherever it occurred. He did, however, reveal his concern to his senior lecturer, Adam Thwaite.

'They're pushing us hard, Adam. Let's hope they soon hit a ceiling. I don't want to be playing catch-up forever. Come what may, we must not become the Faculty of English.'

5

Relationships

(1)

History's course on 'Shakespeare to Shaw: the Historical Background' was set to run for the first time in October 1954. And young Tanya Jenkins was committed to giving three of the early lectures – on the Elizabethan and Stuart periods, straight after Professor Grey's opening lecture.

Tanya was being asked to set first Shakespeare and then Milton in period. This was of course a considerable responsibility for a novice, and she was anxious about it. To lecture about Shakespeare was especially testing. Even the specialists had to admit how, for arguably the world's greatest writer, much about his life and work remains unknown. Even so, the young students in front of her would be expecting clarity in her lectures, with few admissions of ignorance.

However, Tanya had come up with one promising thought. She would present Shakespeare as a Stratford grammar-school boy who had made good. Such a gloss would resonate with her audience. She knew that most of the students in front of her would themselves be grammar-school products, and such an approach would mean something to them.

Dick Rogers, her counterpart in English, had agreed that this would be a good way of introducing the bard to a young audience. Dick also thought up a tempting title:

'Shakespeare: the boy and the man in his time'. And he had suggested some good opening lines:

> Shakespeare is timeless, and the English course will try to suggest why. In contrast, I want to show you today how, despite this timeless quality, he was a man of his time. Is this contradictory? Not really. For Shakespeare's personal experience fed into his timeless writing. He did not produce his great thoughts in a vacuum.

Tanya was very grateful for this help. But Dick had his own concerns – not about his lectures but about his future. Could he hope for a permanent lectureship at Blackchester? He had agreed with Tanya that he must raise the subject with his Professor, and fortunately Mellors had proved to be quite responsive.

'Early days yet, Dick. But I see what you mean. I hope to defeat History on the lectureship front. Keeping you on would fit into that.'

Dick reported Mellors's precise words to Tanya. This was unwise. Dick did not seem to realise that Tanya would feel bound to pass on the 'defeat' remark to her Professor. She did so a few days later. Andrew Grey bristled.

'Thank you, Tanya. Typical of English. A permanent post for Dick Rogers would be a bit like Hitler being given the Sudetanland in 1938. Just about plausible in itself. But Mellors would still expect the same number of new lectureships to follow soon afterwards.'

On hearing this hostile response, Tanya was instantly sorry that she had spoken. It sounded as if her Professor was likely to block the giving of a lectureship to her boyfriend, regardless of his merits. Another lesson for her in academic politics.

But things were inevitably running into choppy waters for each of them. The tension between their respective subjects was forcing both of them to think hard about how much they valued their relationship. Mellors had thrown in just one qualification in conversation with young Dick:

'I hear you're very friendly with History's Tanya Jenkins. Fair enough. But you do know she has a vivid imagination? That she read what may have been a friendly kiss as an assault.'

Rather to his own surprise, Dick improvised a safe answer:

'Ah yes. But whatever happened at Tom's party, Daniel, it's a pity it ever happened.'

In this way the sharpness of his Professor's point was blunted; but without seeming to contradict. Perhaps Dick was learning to be an academic politician more quickly than Tanya.

She received some shrewd guidance from Adam Thwaite. Always perceptive and understanding, he revealed that he recognised her difficulty, while at the same time issuing a warning.

'We historians are happy that you've found a good friend in Dick Rogers. But he is of course a member of the English department. So do not make things difficult for him by telling him anything significant about the thinking of the historians.'

This was of course an adroit way of warning Tanya while seeming to show concern for her boyfriend. By the spring of 1954 she was agonising daily about Dick. She asked herself, 'Does he rate getting the lectureship above caring for me? Of course he does. Best for me to accept this and gently ease off. That solves the problem. I would not want him to lose the lectureship. It would be bad for him. But also it would be bad for me, since such a blow might even tie me into an engagement which I do not necessarily want. I would feel under an obligation.'

Dick, for his part, realised that his desire for the lectureship was overriding. Slowly, he came to accept that he might gain the lectureship and lose Tanya. So be it. She started to be active socially without him, not immediately with other men but with other girls. Both Tanya and Dick had gradually concluded that their relationship could not be 'all for love'.

So they were drifting apart. And Professor Mellors, the head of English, was ultimately the cause. But if he was a destroyer of love, he was also a beneficiary. In the spring of 1954 he had announced that he was to marry Loretta Poulson, formerly the History secretary. She had recently resigned from the History department, quite unexpectedly and without publicly saying why.

In the previous summer the small Primitive Methodist chapel where she worshipped had closed down, and she had switched to the bigger Methodist church in town. This was attended by Daniel Mellors, and their paths had immediately crossed on the first Sunday. Mellors had welcomed her warmly.

'Glad to see you here, Loretta, although of course sorry that your place had to close.'

'Hello, Professor Mellors. I'd expected to see you here. I knew that you were a leading light.'

'Call me Daniel, please. This is not the university. In fact, it makes quite a relaxing contrast. We've quite a few university people here. I know you helped to run the Primitive chapel. I'll introduce you to our people so that you can help us.'

Daniel Mellors was as good as his word, and this helped to develop their connection. They met regularly at services, and on the second occasion he invited Loretta back to his flat for lunch afterwards. Very quickly Christian friendliness began to grow into something more. They found during the autumn and winter of 1953–4 that they were falling in love.

And it eventually became clear why Loretta had resigned from the History department. She had leaked secrets from History to English. At first, she had said little about the historians to Mellors, but increasingly he saw a chance to gain useful information about History's plans. He was clever enough never to ask too obviously. But gradually he knew all that she knew. She was a woman in her thirties, vulnerable, late in love.

The historians had begun to notice how surprisingly often English seemed to have early knowledge of their hopes and fears. How to explain this? In February 1954 Andrew Grey decided to set a trap. He told Loretta that the Historical Association intended to sponsor two scholarships at Blackchester – one in History, one in any other Arts subject apart from English. He included this last exclusion deliberately in order to irritate Mellors. Grey knew that it would ensure that – if Mellors heard about it – he would pass the contents of the leak on to his colleagues.

But the whole thing was a fiction, deliberately invented by Grey. He carefully spoke about the supposed scholarships to no one except Loretta, either at the university or at home. He waited to see what would happen. And within a week, news of the HA's supposed generous offer was circulating on campus.

So there could be no doubt that Loretta had told all to the Professor of English. This particular instance did not matter in itself. But could she be trusted for the future with more sensitive information? The History Professor decided to put the point to her in the starkest terms:

'You've heard from me nearly everything about History's hopes and fears. More even than some of our lecturers. I've assumed that you were one of us. English is our rival – "friendly rival" maybe. It's now obvious that you've been talking too freely to Daniel Mellors. That explains why English seems to have been so well informed in advance about much of our recent thinking.'

Grey might have waited for some sort of excuse at this point. But he had decided in advance to be ruthless:

'So can we now trust one another? Can we work together in the future?'

Loretta made no answer, but she was becoming tearful. Grey pressed on:

'I fear not. I'm sorry it has come to this, for you've been an excellent secretary until now. Perhaps you've found yourself in an impossible situation – caught between two Professors. A pity. But it must be best – for you as much as for me – if you now move on.'

Secretaries were entitled to six months' notice, but Loretta left at the end of the term with six months' salary. The Italian departmental secretary (who was not over-worked) acted as a temporary replacement until a new appointment was made. Loretta's eventual successor was safely married, and in her fifties.

The other historians had of course shared in their Professor's distress at the persistent leaks. In casual conversation they asked one another flippantly how they might strike back. Perhaps some History sympathiser should try to seduce the English secretary! The snag, they admitted unkindly to one another, was that 'she has a face like a brick wall. No wonder Mellors has not been tempted there!'

But why had he not married sooner? In recent years it had even begun to be hinted nudgingly that he was not interested in the opposite sex. In reality, he had almost married just before he came to Blackchester; but the girl had died in a flu epidemic. Maybe this misfortune had encouraged his occasional brusqueness.

The wedding ceremony duly took place in King Street Methodist church at Whitsun 1954. There was of course a large attendance of fellow-Methodists who knew the couple; while from the university all the Blackchester English staff and their wives were invited. Likewise the Dean and his wife. But none of the History staff.

Andrew Grey was surprised by this. Did it mean that the

newly-wed couple did not want to be asked to dinner at the Greys? Loretta had been there often enough when she was departmental secretary; and even Daniel Mellors had been invited when necessary. Now love seemed to have brought not sunshine but frost to Faculty social relationships.

(2)

Tanya Jenkins's new 'Shakespeare to Shaw' part-one lectures were of course due to be given for the first time during the next academic year, 1954–5. By then students such as Mary and Joan would have passed into History part two, and Michael and Andy into part-two English. Provided of course that they passed their respective part-one examinations in the summer of 1954. But most students passed.

Mary Parker's relationship with Michael Young had coasted along through the summer term, but neither had measured its depth. The 1954 long vacation duly came and in July as planned the pair went on a ten-day holiday to the Lake District. Yet, away from the familiar surroundings of the Blackchester campus, they found themselves less comfortable with one another than they had anticipated.

Their love-making at Blackchester had not progressed quite the whole way, partly because both were still virgins. Mary had been ignorantly fearful of pregnancy, and Michael did not really know what he wanted. Sleeping in the youth hostels was of course segregated, but they could have made as much love as they chose on their walks through the hills. In the event, despite this opportunity, they progressed no further, and this left each of them vaguely dissatisfied with one another even though they did not quite realise why.

So when they returned to Blackchester in October 1954 they were both ready for new experiences with fresh people. And also for the stimulus of new courses. Mary had chosen very particularly in this regard. History honours students were allowed to take one course from another department in their second or third years. This course was then examined along with their History courses at the end of their third year. Mary had heard about Tom Tongue's lively lectures, and so she decided to take one of his specialist courses in her second year. He ran it in alternate years, so it was now or never for Mary. It was called 'Politics in Modern English Literature, 1900–50'. It was very much linked to Tom's Marxism, which meant that he taught it with especial enthusiasm. This further recommended him to Mary as the course progressed.

Mary had naturally heard about the 'bite scandal' in her first-year, and had vaguely sympathised with Tanya Jenkins, the young History lecturer. But after getting to know Tom Tongue personally she had changed her mind. She now decided that it was probably unfair to blame him solely and unreservedly. It was probably a misunderstanding. Perhaps Tanya was more innocent than her years might suggest. Mary knew her only by sight, not having been taught by her in the first year.

Tom started to invite Mary to his student parties, which he gave most Saturdays at his home. Except, that is, when he was giving a 'grown-up' party like the one that had involved Tanya. At the first student party of term Tom treated Mary as just one of the group taking his course; but on her second visit in week three the relationship became more personal. At about eleven o'clock, as the party was breaking up, he suddenly asked her if she would stay behind to help him 'tidy up'. She was surprised, but pleased to be asked. She knew that it meant that he had particularly noticed her. But how much? He had talked to her and smiled a lot during the parties, but he had talked and smiled in the same way to other girls. In truth, he was looking for a new attachment. Of course, his amorous reputation was known to everyone. Was it that he was a Marxist free-lover, or was it that he really liked women – and plenty of them liked him, at least in the short-term? Probably both.

Mary now knew enough about men to recognise that Tom was paying her especial attention, and that it was not just about tidying up the room and doing the washing-up. At first on the crucial evening this kept them occupied. Tom washed the glasses and china and Mary dried. This meant that Tom was physically prevented from touching Mary. But he was preparing the ground by cheerful chatter. He was not quite drunk, but he was certainly well-oiled. Mary, for her part, had drunk more than she was used to.

When the last of the glasses had been washed and put away, Tom started to make coffee.

'You must be tired. Sit on the sofa. We can have a calming drink.'

Mary could scarcely object to such a proposal. But she was at least half-aware that by staying longer on her own, and by sitting on the sofa, she was making a commitment. She was allowing herself to be exposed to physical love-making, and maybe more than just a first kiss. Yet she sat down.

Tom set a pot of coffee and two mugs on a small table which he placed in front of the sofa.

'How do you like it? Strong or milky? Add the milk as you like. Sugar?'

Mary added milk generously. Tom sat down beside her.

'I get the impression that you're enjoying the course.'

'Oh, yes. You know so much.'

This personalised the conversation very conveniently for Tom's purpose, even quicker than he had intended.

'Maybe. But I need responsive students to draw me out. And you are one of the most responsive.'

Mary smiled.

'You ask questions, which is good. I don't like students who sit silent, and just write down my words.'

Mary blushed slightly, which made the smooth pale skin of

her face even more tempting. Tom was unlikely to resist such temptation. He therefore plunged boldly in, speaking mainly in monosyllables which unconsciously added to the effect of his words:

'You must know that I like you a lot. I hope you like me. This is the first time we've been on our own together. I want to know you much more.' He paused briefly. 'Of course, I've known lots of girl students down the years. It must be hundreds if not thousands. But I've never made love to any of them. You may find that hard to believe.'

Mary blushed again, but this time more relaxed; and this time she spoke. 'I don't know about that. You do have quite a reputation. I remember the Tanya Jenkins business. But I think that was exaggerated.'

Tom was of course very glad to hear that Mary thought so. It meant that the 'bite crisis' was no obstacle. He decided that now was the moment for a gentle initiative. He lent forward and kissed Mary gently and firmly but quite briefly on the lips.

She responded ever so slightly, moving into the kiss. Good. But even though they were side-by-side on the sofa, Tom realised that this was not the moment to try more. He stifled any such intention, and decided to play it long. He would let Mary go away touched no further. Such restraint would leave her time to think. He sensed that next time she would respond – timidly maybe (for he guessed that she was still a virgin), but fully.

He looked at the clock. 'God, is that the time? Past your hall's midnight deadline. Fortunately I know the porters. I was going to come back with you anyhow.'

Mary was now likely to go to every one of Tom's Saturday parties – with the excuse of being there early and late to help him with the preparation and clearing up. Of course, she was also hearing Tom in his weekly course seminar. He spoke there to a dozen students; but somehow she warmed to his words as if they were being addressed directly to her – not because she understood or accepted all his arguments, but because of his almost boyish enthusiasm. The way he spoke made him seem younger than his forty years. His claims were unlimited: 'Marx will one day be recognised as a second Jesus Christ.'

All the students had been given a list of essay titles. They were each to write one essay by mid-term. So in due course Mary could expect to meet Tom to discuss her essay. Here was a vital academic contact. But their social contact was going to be much more continuous.

On the next Saturday they finished up again sitting side-by-side on the sofa. Tom kissed her still gently, but this time repeatedly, and he was glad to find that she responded at least sufficiently. But he was still cautious about how far he went, brushing her breasts casually but without fondling. And once more he used the lateness of the hour as an excuse to stop.

'Midnight again. I hope it's not the same porter. He'll be jumping to conclusions.'

Tom said this last deliberately, hinting for Mary's benefit that there would indeed soon be conclusions.

These duly followed on the next Saturday.

They sat as before on the sofa, and each drank some coffee. Tom then leant over and kissed Mary gently; but he did not linger. Instead he pulled back immediately. Paradoxically, this was meant not as a sign of restraint but as a hint that there was much more to come. Instinctively, Mary understood. She could have stood up, and said that she must go. But she did not.

A minute later Tom leant over and finally took her firmly in his arms. She did not resist. Instead she closed her eyes, and waited. What followed need not be detailed. Sufficient to say that Mary stayed the night and was a virgin no longer.

And paradoxically by not returning to her room until after

breakfast (rather than after midnight) she had no problem with the porter.

Her problem was with herself. At Tom's house she had been carried along by his love-making; but when she got back to her room she inevitably started to ask herself what was happening. Not only *what* but also *should it be?* Weren't lecturers forbidden from having relationships with students – just like doctors and patients?

Yet Mary felt pleased as well as worried. She did not feel guilty that she had given herself to him. She was tacitly accepting that, while the initiative was entirely Tom's, she had been a willing party. His step-by-step approach each Saturday had been clear enough. She could have simply stayed away. But what, she wondered, would happen next? Presumably their relationship must remain secret. That might be difficult. Her fellow-students would notice any too-frequent contact. Yet she hoped to see him every day.

While Mary was uncertain, Tom was not. He had planned what had happened. And he was pleased to have succeeded. But why, he now asked himself, had he broken his long-standing rule not to harass students? No matter how attractive they might be. Perhaps, he admitted to himself, it had been because there was usually some older woman in tow, or at least in prospect, whereas currently there had been no one for some weeks. Not a comfortable explanation.

But what should he do now? Call it all off? Explain to Mary that it was against the rules? But she might then turn against him, and complain to the authorities. His career would be shattered. In any case, he liked the girl quite a lot – found her appealing. He did not want to give her up immediately. So he concluded that it would be both safer and more pleasant to continue with the affair at least for the time being. Best not to try to think too far ahead. It might eventually fizzle out with no harm done on either side.

So he sent a note to Mary asking her to meet him that

afternoon in his office in the English department. That would be the safest place to be seen together, because it was where they might be talking about an essay. Tom's actual purpose was to discuss with Mary how they could safely meet in future.

'We must be careful not to be seen too much together.'

'Oh, yes. I was wondering what to do.'

'Saturday parties fine. But if you were never in your own room overnight it would be noticed sooner or later. Perhaps we could risk one night in the week.'

So that was how it was through the rest of the term until early December.

Neither said anything to the other about the wider impropriety of their relationship. This amounted to recognition by both of them that, short of ending it completely, they could not speak to much purpose – unless of course they declared their 'love' for one another. And Tom knew that he was not in love, while inexperienced Mary simply did not know whether she was in love or not.

However, she did raise one point of concern. 'I don't want to get pregnant.' But she acquiesced readily enough when Tom answered reassuringly, 'Have no fear. I'll use something.'

This reassurance overlooked the fact that he had not done so on the sofa. The implication was that it would not matter.

(3)

But it did matter. By the end of term early in December 1954 Mary was getting worried. She had missed a period, and there was no sign of it recurring. What should she do? Who should she tell? Her friend Joan perhaps; but Joan would expect to be given the name of her boyfriend. And the fact that he was a member of staff, not a fellow student, would make a difference. Joan would probably express shock rather than simply surprise. She came from a strict Christian family, and might even insist upon telling their History Professor.

So Mary told no one on campus before she left for the Christmas vacation – not even Tom. She had decided against telling him until she had talked to her parents. As soon as she got back home in Sheffield she went to see her GP, still in the hope that it might be a false alarm. But his examination and tests soon made it clear that she was probably several weeks pregnant.

'You have decisions to make, Mary. What do you know about the father and his family? Do you marry him, or not? If not, what do you do once the baby has been born? Do you send it for adoption?'

The doctor felt bound to list all the questions. He was assuming that the father was a fellow student.

'I take it you'll tell your parents very soon. You need to know what they think – how helpful they're going to be. They'll be shocked at first – that's natural. As an only child you are at the centre of their thoughts. But you must hope that after a few hours or days they'll become supportive and will help you decide what to do. By the start of next term you must have come to some conclusions. One choice will be whether you want to continue at university – or give up, at least for this year.'

The doctor now paused, for he could see that Mary was becoming tearful. So far she had borne up surprisingly well, even while telling no one. Until she heard the plain truth in the surgery, she had not quite accepted the reality. But now she knew that the crisis time had come. At last she must tell her parents something. She decided that she would speak to her mother first. She would do so immediately on return from the doctor's, in the hope that they might then share in cushioning the shock to her father on his return from work that evening.

But it didn't work out like that.

When told: 'I'm just back from the doctor. He says I'm probably pregnant,' her mother collapsed in tears, barely able to respond. When chokingly she did finally answer, what she said did not help at all. Instead, it brought the additional question of the child's father straight into the reckoning.

'What do you mean? You can't be pregnant. You haven't even got a boyfriend, now that you've given up Michael. Or is he the father after all?'

Last term Mary had of course said nothing to her parents about her relationship with a senior lecturer in English. She had hoped to hold this back at first, while they talked about the pregnancy separately. She had not foreseen that such a silence was never likely to work for more than a few minutes since everyone, on being told, always assumed that the father was a fellow student. In correcting this, Mary was bound to admit at least part of the truth to her mother– that the father was not Michael but an academic, even if she did not name him.

She now decided that her original intention of telling her father with help from her mother was a non-starter. When he came home, her mother was still in shock, sitting red-eyed in a chair. It was Mary who had prepared the evening meal. She waited for her father to freshen up in the bathroom and to come into the dining room and to sit at the table.

'Dad. Bad news, I'm afraid. I went to see Dr Smith this morning, and he says that almost certainly I'm pregnant. It will be confirmed by further tests. I'm sorry.'

To say sorry was of course grossly inadequate. Yet what else could she say? Her father, who doted upon his daughter, caught his breath. He was a mild-mannered man, but of course he was shocked. So his face registered at first shock – and then disappointment. Disappointment was of course better from Mary's point of view than straight anger, which might have been destructive. Instead, his questioning, although not immediately forgiving, soon became positive.

'Good God! You mean you're going to have a child? Oh Mary, I thought you had more sense.'

His face drained of colour, but his thinking remained clear. His love for his daughter prevailed. He swallowed, and after a few seconds he came up with three linked questions: 'What about the father? What does he think? Is he in your year?'

If she had been able to say that the father was a fellow student, such an answer would have begun to move the discussion on from a question of guilt and blame to one of ways and means. It would have introduced the possibility of marriage, which would of course have been a signpost towards near-normality.

Instead, Mary felt even more vulnerable. She had no escape from admitting that the father was not a fellow student.

'Not a student! Who the hell is it?'

'One of the lecturers.'

Her father reeled in his chair. But she refused to say who it was, or how old he was. She claimed not to know his precise age. She revealed that she had not yet told the father, and that she had wanted to talk at home first. This delay reduced her feeling of vulnerability in front of her parents, for it showed that she was still in charge of the timetable. She announced that she would go to Blackchester the next day to see the child's father. Fortunately, it was only a couple of hours' train journey from Sheffield.

Her father responded: 'I'll go with you. I want to meet this man.'

Such a meeting was the last thing Mary wanted at present. Fortunately, she managed to think up a neat holding answer:

'Yes, of course you must meet him. I'll go to Blackchester tomorrow, and I'll bring him back.'

Reluctantly, Mary's parents agreed to this timetable. They assumed that it meant that they would meet the father the next day, or at the latest the following day. But in fact Mary had not promised any such thing.

She went by train back to Blackchester next morning, ten days before Christmas. She had not dared to phone Tom from home, but she did so briefly from a call-box at Sheffield station. She still did not tell him why she was returning, only that she had 'urgent news'. He duly met her on arrival at Blackchester, and they drove straight to his house in his car. On the way she still refused to say what was so 'urgent'.

'Wait till we get to your place.'

So Tom held back until they were sitting on the fateful sofa. In fact, he had fearfully guessed the truth:

'Mary, are you pregnant? Is that why you've returned?'

'Yes. My doctor guesses about two months.'

He looked surprised, even though he had expected the answer. He knew that he had been 'careful' – apart from their first time. Damn.

'Oh Mary, it's my fault. We've been unlucky. It must have been that very first time.'

Mary simply nodded and said 'Yes'.

There was a brief silence as they sat side-by-side – thinking. But Tom soon realised that there was no point in feeling sorry for themselves. They must decide what to do. So he kissed her gently on the cheek and followed up with a sensitive but nonetheless pointed question.

'Do you want to have the child?'

Tom realised that Mary's answer would point towards one of three courses – abortion, marriage, adoption.

'Yes. I think so.' She paused. 'Maybe. But it depends. What do *we* want?'

Tom immediately sensed that these last innocent-sounding words carried an implication of marriage. But he knew that he was not 'in love' with Mary; and so, while not immediately ruling marriage out, he was unwilling to be hurried into it.

'Let's think things through. You don't have to have the child, if you don't want to.'

'What do you mean?'

'You could have an abortion. It would be no great problem so early in the pregnancy.'

Mary winced. She had barely thought about abortion. Marriage? A possibility. Adoption? An alternative possibility. She was aware that abortion was illegal, and that it was a back-street business.

Tom said that he knew 'someone in town' who could do it. What he did not say was that a former girlfriend of his had employed the woman's services a couple of years earlier.

On hearing the abortion proposal Mary stiffened. The very mention made her mind up for her. She realised that she did *not* want an abortion – whatever else happened, she did not want to kill her child.

Tom sensed the strength of her reaction, and abandoned the idea. He knew that if she had been agreeable, it would have avoided all need to think about marriage. But now he accepted that marriage was top of the list – her list, if not his.

He was still cool on the idea. He knew that his attachment to Mary was probably only a passing fancy. She had a pleasant outgoing personality, and was pretty enough. Maybe she was 'in love' with him. Yet she had never quite said so, and he had certainly not spoken of love to her. For him it had all the makings of an affair – something which would flourish for a while and then no doubt fade. He now found that this was not necessarily how Mary saw it.

Even before she knew that she was pregnant, she had begun to feel more deeply. She was not certain quite what she felt, but she told herself (although not Tom) that she might have come to love him. She was waiting for some encouragement in that direction. But he had deliberately said nothing so serious. In his own eyes he was a free spirit, a perpetual bachelor. He had twice broken off affairs at Blackchester when the woman had started to get too serious.

But could he do so now, with Mary pregnant?

He felt uneasy. This was something very unusual for him, so unlike the Marxist certainty in his political life.

'I take it then that you're ready to have the child?'

This was of course an obvious conclusion in the absence of abortion. But was the birth to be preceded by marriage? Marriage would end their crisis after a fashion, although nothing could alter the fact that Tom was twice Mary's age and her teacher. The publicity for the university would be bad.

Tom dared not risk saying the words 'We could get married'. He sensed that, if he did, Mary would hear them not as something for discussion but as a firm proposal. And she would probably accept.

He therefore leapt over the question of marriage by raising the possibility of the child being adopted. Tom intended it as a clever shift of thought, by-passing the idea of marriage altogether. But Mary saw the implication immediately, and refused to be diverted. Tom had not mentioned marriage, so she did so now herself. And significantly her tone became much sharper:

'What about us getting married? Why do you not mention marriage? I thought it was the man who made the proposal.'

Tom winced. Her sharpened tone made him realise that the problem was his as well as hers. If she became publicly hostile on campus his reputation would be seriously damaged. His affairs with fellow members of the academic or secretarial staff had been more or less indulged as private (or not so private) business. But indulgence would not be shown over an affair with a student – certainly not if he refused to marry the student. Would he be able to stay at Blackchester?

Tom found himself improvising as best he could, trying hard to avoid sounding either positive or negative.

'We must be careful for both our sakes. Would marriage work?'

He tried to use the difference in their ages and situations as a defence: 'We have not known each other very long. I'm twice your age. How will the university react?'

His language was of course much too condensed – indeed, it was almost garbled. Tom was not in control of his thinking. He was reacting awkwardly to the crisis. He should have been much slower, more sympathetic. Worst of all, he seemed too guarded.

Mary's response to Tom now became incisive, almost hostile. Unsurprisingly, her answer was child-centred. Tom, never a family man, had completely failed to foresee Mary's maternal reaction.

'You say that we must think about the best for ourselves. Surely our first concern must be to secure a good childhood for our child. That's what matters most. We can think about ourselves when that's settled.'

Mary's tone had become almost cold, with no hint of residual deference towards Tom. It was the mother speaking, not the student. It made all the difference. She had grown up all of a sudden.

Tom sensed this change, and shuddered internally. He felt and looked slightly lost, very different from his usual fluent self. He started to answer, but with no persuasiveness. He was rambling.

'Yes, I suppose so. I see that. But we don't have to decide anything. At least, not today. We can wait …' Pause. 'Let's …'

But Mary gave him no time for any more rambling. She had not been intending to go back to Sheffield that night; she had assumed that they would have sorted out their relationship sufficiently for her to stay at Tom's. But now she cut in bluntly, and with great perception: 'We don't know what to do. We don't really know our own minds. The one thing certain is that we're not agreed. We'll have to think further, and then talk again.'

Tom did not argue. 'Maybe you're right.' He knew that he needed some space to think, space without Mary. Of course, they must meet and talk again. There were only a few days left before Christmas, and it would be a fortnight before everything was over. He was scheduled to spend a few days with his elderly parents in London: there seemed to be no point in cancelling that, although he would say nothing to them about the pregnancy.

'Suppose you come here again between Christmas and New Year? By then we'll have had more time to think. I'll be back here by Tuesday the twenty-eighth. Phone me.'

On this neutral note they parted. Mary did not stay for a meal, not even for coffee. 'If I go straightaway I can catch the 12.30.' He drove her back to the station almost in silence. Mary had been in Blackchester for not much more than an hour – much less than that at Tom's house. She was back home in Sheffield by a quarter to four.

Her parents had of course expected her to bring the father. While on the train, she had thought out how best to explain his absence. She would explain frankly what had happened – that she had failed to agree anything with him. She decided that her default position was now to talk the whole thing through with her parents. It would help her to clear her mind, and would probably rally their support.

'We've settled nothing. He seemed to be keen for abortion. I ruled that out. Adoption came up, but he was reluctant even to consider marriage. I was surprised by his whole tone, and began to get critical. Quite quickly it became clear that our safest course for now is to admit that we're not ready to make any decisions. That's why I've come back so soon. You may be able to help.'

These words of course brought her parents right into the discussion. Her father responded supportively: 'I hope so.

No use pretending that it's not a mess, but it simply has to be sorted. With the minimum of hurt to you and to the child. If the father ends up getting hurt in some way, so be it.'

Mary nodded, offering no defence of Tom. Her father continued: 'But we do need to know something about him. Let's hope he's not married. That would only add to the mess.'

'No, he's not married.'

'What's his name?'

Mary replied unthinkingly, not realising that by naming him she left him exposed, out of her protection. 'Tom Tongue. He's a senior lecturer in English.'

'Presumably, if he's a full-time lecturer, he has some means. He would be able to support the child?'

'Yes.'

'Good. That applies even if there's no marriage.'

Mary's mother cut in briefly, wringing her hands: 'I just don't know whether I want them to marry, or not.'

Her husband responded: 'Nor do I, till I've seen the father. The one certainty is that we don't want an abortion.'

Mary agreed: 'I told him I didn't want that.'

Her father bristled: 'He was prepared to murder his own child? Not a recommendation for a future husband.'

The conversation rambled on for the rest of the evening, and intermittently every day over the Christmas week-end. Relatives visited, but Mary and her parents contrived to say nothing about her pregnancy. Being forced to think about something else was probably good for them.

By Tuesday the 28th every angle had been explored. Abortion – definitely out. Adoption – possible as a last resort. But only just. The fixed truth was that Mary's parents did not want to lose their grandchild. And that thought was becoming a strong influence.

Mary could of course simply choose to keep the child as an unmarried mother. But that would tarnish all three of them, plus the child. So, despite her parents' doubts about Tom as a person, were they being drawn towards wanting Mary and Tom to marry? Maybe.

(4)

Mary told her parents that Tom had suggested another meeting soon after the 28th.

'I'll phone him this evening, and go tomorrow'.

Her father agreed, but insisted on going with her. 'I want to weigh up this man. The sort of person he is must influence whether we want you to marry him.'

Mary had hoped to go on her own, but she knew that her father had every right to go; and as she was under twenty-one his permission for marriage was needed by law. There was also the advantage that they could drive over in the family car.

'All right. But I must have some time with Tom on my own. If you come, you must stay outside in the car while we talk in private in hope of settling something, something good. Then you can come in to meet Tom and hear how things are.'

This was an unexpected course of action, but Mary's father decided that it could do no further harm.

'Very well. I'll hold back for a few minutes, in hopes that you can make progress. But what will "progress" be? Until I've weighed up this Tom Tongue – what sort of person he is – I can't know what would be best.'

So they drove over the next morning, stopping in a lay-by near Blackchester for Mary to freshen up. She was wearing one of her best skirt-and-blouse outfits. She was pale, but clear-minded, determined this time to come to a conclusion, and hopeful that it would be a good one.

The car stopped outside Tom's house, and Mary got out. She went up the drive and rang the bell. Meanwhile, her father drove some distance down the road. He intended to return in about ten minutes. They had agreed that if Tom knew that he was outside he would insist upon calling Mary's father in, and such a premature meeting would prevent the vital tête-à-tête.

Tom waved Mary in, pecked her on the cheek (but no more), and pointed towards the sofa. This time Tom took care to make coffee before they said anything important. But first Mary had to explain away her unexpected arrival:

'I got an earlier train, and then a bus.'

Tom did not question the lie. 'I was planning to meet the same train as last week. How are you feeling? I mean physically.'

'Oh, OK. The doctor examined me.'

Had Tom made this his first question out of genuine concern? We must presume so. But he cannot have forgotten that a miscarriage would solve everything.

'Have you had any fresh thoughts?' he asked.

'My parents were shocked at first of course, but we've since talked about everything several times over. They assumed that the father was a student, and were extra alarmed when I told them it was a lecturer. They're still very questioning about you. They want to know what sort of person you are.'

Tom sensed that this was because they were assessing him as a prospective son-in-law. He realised that he would have to be very careful not to get into a position where, if Mary's parents expressed approval (or at least acceptance) of him, marriage became inevitable. He was simply not prepared to allow them to exercise the last word.

'Fair enough that they want to know me. But their attitude cannot be decisive. It's we two who must decide what we want.'

Such an emphasis sounded reasonable, and yet it was immediately worrying for Mary. She realised that once again he was backing away from discussing marriage; he was using her parents as cover. This made her suddenly tense. She stiffened, and in her irritation, she grasped the nettle in a very few words:

'For the child's sake I think we should get married.'

Tom winced, but did not immediately answer. So Mary developed her point temptingly:

'When I say "for the child's sake" that doesn't need to be the only reason. If we are in love that would be a strong reason in itself.'

Tom stiffened. He was still evasive, answering only 'yes'.

This time Mary went the whole hog by asking the vital question and in the simplest terms. Her face was set. 'Are we in love?'

Tom could have said: 'Of course we are'. That would have been the most positive response. It would have shifted the discussion from 'should we marry?' to the very different '*when* should we marry?'

Mary sensed that they had reached the crunch point. If Tom persisted in being evasive it would be unbearable. If his response sounded loving, all would be well: anything less would be insufficient.

Tom visibly hesitated. He knew that he had never intended to marry this girl. 'Love' had not been in his mind.

'I don't know. "Love" is such an elusive thing. We've not needed to think about it till now.'

True enough for him. Yet even before she knew about the pregnancy Mary had begun to wonder whether she was in love with Tom. She now heard his words – still so guarded and so careful – and burst into uncontrollable tears.

'You don't love me! You only love yourself!'

That was it! She did not want to hear any more, brief though their present exchanges had been. She sprang up and ran into the hall, snatching her coat from a peg and reaching the door. Tom ran after her.

'Mary. Don't go. We've got to be calm. We must be sensible.'

But for Mary the dam had burst. She ran down the drive to the car, which had just come back. When her father saw her in distress, he sprang out from the driver's seat. But before he could get round, Mary had jumped into the front seat. Tom was on the pavement.

Mary's father spat out, 'You must be Tom Tongue. You're a disgrace. No point in talking to you. I shall complain to the university.'

Tom tried to answer, but Mary's father ran straight back into the car and drove noisily away.

At first Mary was still in tears. Her father, although upset, swallowed hard and spoke gently:

'No need to tell me what happened till you feel calmer, Mary. Clearly, any dealings with Tom Tongue are over. I've told him that I'll complain to the university. Writing to Blackchester will help us to think straight.'

After a few miles, Mary explained what had happened.

'He made it clear that he did not love me, and had not even thought about it. That was what made me snap – not even to have thought about it.'

'Well, that rules out marriage. Your mother and I had begun to take marriage as a serious possibility, if we'd found him to be tolerable as a person. Clearly, he's a predator. An ageing predator by the look of him.'

This point about age was the last nail in the coffin as far as Mary's father was concerned. It could never be a normal marriage.

When they got back to Sheffield Mary's father gave her mother a quick outline of what had happened. She sensibly insisted that Mary should go up to her bedroom for a lie-down. The baby mattered more than Tom Tongue.

What to do next? Mary's father was a solicitor's clerk, which meant that he was well qualified to write to the Vice Chancellor.

'You say the university is closed all this week. So I'll aim to get a letter to him by early next week. That will give us plenty of time to compose our letter. Whatever we decide about Mary, Tom Tongue must not be allowed to get away with it.'

So that was how they proceeded. They could afford to delay briefly over making decisions for Mary, while they decided how best to expose Tom Tongue.

Dear Vice Chancellor,

My daughter, Mary Parker, is a second-year History student, and I find myself having to write to you about a most serious matter relating to her.

I find that during last term she started to have a sexual relationship with one of her teachers – Tom Tongue, a senior lecturer in English. She is taking his 'Politics in Modern English Literature' course.

Such a relationship between a student and one of her teachers is of course improper, even if not actually illegal, and I would have been writing to you as soon as I heard about it. Unfortunately, I now have to do so even more urgently. My daughter has revealed that her doctor recently told her that she is pregnant with this man's child. What has happened at the university is therefore now extremely serious.

What is your view about the matter? Various courses of action are possible. I will simply tell you here that at first we were hesitantly inclined to encourage the couple to marry; but that this has now been ruled out by Mary, after she found to her dismay that Tom Tongue had never given such a possibility any thought.

Rather than go into further details in a letter, I think it desirable for us to meet to discuss this deplorable business further. You will be anxious to minimize the damage to the good name of the university, while I am of course most anxious to protect my daughter's future.

Yours sincerely,
Edward Parker

PS. I am sending copies of this letter to the Professors of History and English.

(5)

The Vice Chancellor received this letter on the Tuesday after New Year, his first day back. His secretary had put it on top of the pile.

'It sounds worrying, Vice Chancellor.'

Roger Walker read the neatly written script.

'God. Yes. It does. We must act at once. I see the Professors of History and English have been sent copies, but not the Dean. Make a copy and send it to him straightaway. I presume he's on campus. If not, try his home. I want to have an early meeting with him – today if possible – before we bring in the two Professors.'

Neither Andrew Grey nor Daniel Mellors were on campus, and their secretaries were still away on holiday, which meant that their respective departments knew nothing that morning about what was looming. The delay suited the Vice Chancellor. It left him free to see the Dean on his own at two o'clock.

'I know of course about the tension already existing between History and English, so I thought we'd better talk first without their Professors. This news is of course appalling – for English and for the university. English is our fastest-growing subject. If this episode attracts bad publicity in the national press, our expansion will suffer.'

Guy Johnson nodded his agreement to each point.

'Oh dear. Tom Tongue has a reputation as a womaniser, but I thought he kept his hands off students. We're bound to talk to him first. To confirm the facts, and then to ask what he intends to do. The letter seems to rule out marriage; but maybe he would now be willing to talk about it. We could then talk to the girl and her parents.'

'Yes. A speedy marriage would of course spare the university most of the bad publicity. It could be presented as no worse than love out of control.'

These were the very practical thoughts of two administrators, thinking only about the good name of the university.

The Vice Chancellor realised that he must immediately arrange a meeting with Mary and her father, and his secretary set up a time for the following Friday afternoon. Meanwhile the university carefully prepared itself.

The Dean decided that he would try to see Tom Tongue the next day, Wednesday, after he had spoken to the two Professors. He would then brief the VC, who would almost certainly want to speak to Tom after the briefing – whether one-to-one or with others present would be for the VC to decide.

Following his meeting with the VC the Dean rang each Professor at home in turn. Since History was the injured party he felt it appropriate to speak to Andrew Grey first.

'Andrew, bad news I'm afraid, which requires us to talk urgently with the VC. I'll read out a letter which he has just received. There is a copy in your post in the department. It is from the father of one of your second-year students, Mary Parker. She's taking a course taught by Tom Tongue.'

The very mention of Tom's name alerted Andrew Grey. When he had heard the contents of the letter he drew in a deep breath:

'Good God. Tom bloody Tongue again. I suppose with anyone else we would still be hoping that it was not all bad – that there must be some respectable explanation. But with Tom Tongue we must assume the worst, and that the good name of the university is in danger. Mind you, my first concern must be with Mary Parker.'

'Yes. You'll want to talk to her on Friday, probably before she and her father see the rest of us. You can be in effect their counsel. I will of course be sympathetic, but as Dean I will try to get Daniel Mellors on side. I must balance concern for the girl with my concern for the Faculty and university. I'll try to check him from rushing to Tom's defence, which might be his first reaction.'

He next rang Daniel Mellors and read him the letter. The Dean was pleased to find that the Professor of English made no attempt to excuse his colleague. His first thought was his department's recruitment campaign.

'This is bad. Tom is well known outside the university. It could do our recruitment immense damage with the schools. We must of course confirm the facts with Tom. But I fear it could be true. What does History think?'

'History' in the person of Andrew Grey was left thinking very hard. Before phoning Mary at home early on the Wednesday morning Grey thought it would be a good idea to enquire about her from her personal tutor, Richard Corke. He was very supportive:

'Oh she's a good student, pleasant, works steadily, has ideas. I reckon she's a safe upper-second – or would have been if Tom Tongue hadn't got his hands on her. I hope he gets the boot!'

'He may do. But not if they marry. At their meeting on Friday the VC and Dean are going to sound that out – despite what is said in the letter.'

Andrew Grey rang Mary and her father at home on the Wednesday morning. Mr Parker, who was off work over the holiday period, answered the phone. Grey emphasised that he did not imagine that anything could be settled at such a distance:

'I just wanted to get in touch, and to convey my sense of shock and sympathy. The Dean will be seeing Tom Tongue as soon as possible. We may know more after that. Things may move on, or they may not. We must meet on Friday before you both see the VC. Whatever happens, I just wanted to explain that I see my role as the advocate for Mary. The VC and Dean will be sympathetic, but of course they have their own horizons.'

'It's good to hear what you say, Professor. We're still a bit in a state of shock. My first concern is of course for Mary. I was half-inclined to favour marriage, but not after Tom Tongue said that he had never even thought about it. That proved how his interest in Mary was purely physical – not pure at all.'

Grey did not disagree, but wondered what the culprit would now say for himself. 'The Dean is seeing Tom Tongue this afternoon. We have of course to give him a chance to explain himself, although the grim fact of the pregnancy cannot be gainsaid. Apparently he's been away, and only gets back this morning. Does Mary want to speak to me?'

She did. 'Thank you for phoning, Professor Grey. I feel guilty for putting the university in such a difficulty.'

'No point in guilt, Mary. We must seek the best solution – for you above all, and for the university next.'

He made no mention of Tom Tongue to Mary, and she likewise did not refer to him. The implication was that no sympathy was owing to someone who had taken advantage of her. It remained to be decided what the consequence of their hostility would be.

Tom went to the Dean's office at two o'clock, having only got back to his home about midday. His cleaning woman, who had been at work in the house all morning, told him that the Dean's secretary had been phoning hourly. When he phoned back, he had asked the secretary why, but she would only say that 'a matter of urgency had come up'.

Her tone led Tom to think that he had better ring up his Professor to find out what was going on. Over the phone Daniel Mellors sounded sharp and cold. He read out Mr Parker's letter.

'They're seeing the VC on Friday afternoon. The Dean will be there, and Andrew Grey and myself. You'll be required to make yourself available on campus. Have you anything to add or subtract?'

This sudden outpouring left Tom reeling. He had to sit down.

At first he was at a loss for words. 'I had no idea … no idea … I thought Mary would get back to me sooner or later, any day, and that we would try again. I suppose her father did say they would complain to the university, but I hardly took that in, at least not as immediate.'

'Well, they *have* complained instanter. Not surprising. And for a start you'll have to explain yourself to the VC. As I understand it, Mary was ready to marry you, and her parents were likely to accept that outcome, but all three are now disgusted because you've made it clear to her that you never even contemplated marriage. They're now hostile to the whole idea.'

Tom hesitated, and could only say 'Oh'.

'This makes the whole business even more serious if it gets out, as it will. It threatens the good name of the university, just when we're trying extra-hard to sell ourselves. A speedy marriage could almost be explained away, but no marriage at all cannot. A squalid affair between a lecturer and a student is just what the popular press likes to deplore.'

The Professor's tone – his use of the word 'squalid' – made Tom Tongue realise that he was on his own. Mellors was a practising Methodist. The English department was not going to defend, or even to explain, its senior lecturer's conduct.

So Tom went to the Dean's office in a daze. He had not had time to catch up with all the developments, let alone to think about them.

The Dean's tone was distant: 'My first task must be to confirm the facts. I take it that you do not dispute that you must be the father.'

'No.'

'That is of course the worst possible news. If it had been a student, it would have been almost excusable. But you are her teacher, the university's representative. You are not even a young lecturer, still in his twenties. Being twice her age makes a bad situation even worse.'

In just five short sentences Guy Johnson had presented the university's crushing case against Tom Tongue.

'Have you any defence to offer? I can't imagine one.'

'Of course I regret what has happened. Not just selfishly for my own sake, but even more for Mary's. I acted without thought. I've let her down. I've let the university down. I've been a fool. What more can I say? If there's anything I can do to reduce the damage I will do it – gladly.'

The Dean was pleased to hear Tom's unqualified contrition. He was equally pleased to hear the mention of damage reduction:

'You're in a hole. And because the university is in danger of very bad publicity, it has decided – that is, the Vice Chancellor and I have decided – to see if we can help you out of it. Not because of any liking for you, but for the university's sake.'

Tom murmured a subdued 'Thank you'.

The Dean spelt out a possible course of action:

'Mr Parker's letter to the Vice Chancellor mentions the question of marriage. The discovery that you had never even vaguely considered it stunned Mary. In her eyes, it showed that your involvement with her had no depth, was purely physical. It is what has now made her so bitter; why she and her father have contacted the Vice Chancellor. She wants nothing more to do with you. But she does want to see you punished – her father even more so.'

Tom Tongue was having his eyes opened. He was beginning to realise why – instead of remaining a matter between themselves – his relationship with Mary had become a university crisis.

'Thank you. I'm beginning to catch up. I must see Mary again. I'll say so to the Vice Chancellor.'

He duly mentioned this intention when he met the VC later that day, with the Dean present. The VC had begun by issuing a formal warning.

'You've abused your relationship with a student. It may lead to your dismissal. However, the outcome remains uncertain. We may be able to find some way out that will reduce the damage to the university.'

'And hopefully also the damage to Mary,' added the Dean.

After saying again what he had said to the Dean about his contrition, Tom asked the VC what he had in mind as the next step.

The VC was clear and emphatic:

'Marriage would defuse the crisis. The university could say that this was only a case of love getting ahead of itself. The letter says that Mary has ruled marriage out because of your attitude. You had (the letter says) "never given it any thought". Could you please now give it some thought and discuss it with Mary?'

Tom could not refuse. To have done so would have virtually meant the end of his career at Blackchester. After refusing to make an offer of marriage, he would have been bound to resign, or be sacked. Yet why should he refuse? To think again and to talk afresh with Mary was so obviously a reasonable course.

It then became a question of how best to approach Mary. The Dean suggested that the Professor of History would be the right person to arrange another meeting between her and Tom. So Andrew Grey duly phoned Mary and her father again that same Wednesday evening.

'Mary, I've a suggestion to make. I want to set up another meeting between you and Tom. I know you've been disgusted by him. But there ought to be one last attempt to defuse the crisis before you meet the Vice Chancellor.'

Mary was surprised by this proposal, but was sufficiently calm to agree, although unenthusiastically:

'Oh. If you really think so. I've nothing more to say to Tom. So it will all be up to him.'

Professor Grey had decided not to mention marriage as a way out. He knew that – much as the university might want it to happen – no one apart from Tom himself was in a position to speak of it as a solution.

(6)

Mary and her father drove over to Blackchester on the Friday morning. They were both in their best clothes, for this was 1955 and it was an important meeting. Mr Parker wore a grey suit, which he had recently worn at a wedding, while Mary was in a smart but not too close-fitting navy-blue dress and coat. Their only concession to informality was that they did not wear hats.

They had arranged with Professor Grey to go to his office by 10.30. He met them there and gave them coffee. The Dean was also present, and explained why:

'I thought it important to meet you, Mr Parker, before this afternoon's gathering with the Vice Chancellor. He will of course be in charge, but no one can anticipate how it will go. Much depends upon this morning's meeting between Mary here and Tom.'

Mary smiled a tense smile, and Andrew Grey thought it wise to chip in:

'You are under no pressure from the university, Mary. The fact that you're talking to Tom once more does not mean that he has the initiative. You decide what you want to do.'

Mary nodded.

'You are of course seeing the Vice Chancellor with your father this afternoon. You may find yourself wanting to report progress to the VC – or you may want simply to hear the university's reaction. I will be there, as will the Dean. Also the Professor of English. So you will have all the interested parties present apart from Tom Tongue. He has been told to be on call.'

Andrew Grey had arranged for the Parkers and Tom to meet in his office at 11.30. They were to be left on their own and undisturbed. Meanwhile, Grey himself went across to the office of the Professor of English. This was a rare visit to his rival, but he thought it desirable to hear the latest English thinking:

'Well, Daniel, have you any suggestions? I am of course especially concerned for Mary and History. You must be concerned for English. But what is your thinking about Tom Tongue?'

Mellors was surprisingly frank about his colleague:

'I will not attempt to defend him. His personal life has been occasioning comment for years, which English could have done without. We have had to live with it. But an affair with a student is indefensible. Maybe he should take himself off whatever the outcome, even marriage.'

Andrew Grey was surprised to hear so firm and forward-looking a comment. What, he asked himself, was Mellors up to? If Tom Tongue went, he would certainly have to be replaced. But did the English Professor intend to try to exploit this vacancy by demanding more than a simple replacement?

Meanwhile Mary and her father sat in the History Professor's office awaiting Tom Tongue. Andrew Grey had ensured that three armchairs were available. At precisely 11.30 Tom walked over from his own office.

'Mr Parker, I'm Tom Tongue. Hello, Mary.'

Mary and her father had stood up at Tom's entry, but they did not extend their hands for a handshake. All three sat down, and Mary's father spoke first:

'The university felt that you and Mary should have one further meeting to discuss this deplorable business. We have agreed. The university is of course concerned about the damage to its reputation. That's as maybe, but my main interest is to find out what's best for Mary.'

Tom made to cut in, but Mr Parker insisted upon continuing. He raised his right hand as he did so.

'We've asked ourselves no end of times what that outcome might be. One solution of sorts would be marriage; and at one point Mary's mother and myself had almost come round to that. But then Mary found out that you had no interest in marriage, only in abortion. It naturally disgusted her – and us.'

After making this barbed comment, Mr Parker stood up.

'That's all I want to say. I'm going to leave you two on your own together. I'm not optimistic, but we shall see.'

He then walked briskly out.

Both Mary and Tom were surprised by this sudden exit, for Mr Parker had said nothing about it in advance to Mary. Probably it was a dramatic spur-of-the-moment decision. It certainly established a clear starting point for discussion between the two principals.

Tom spoke first:

'I can understand why your father feels shocked by all this, Mary. I would do so in his place. But we are where we are. I've been thinking hard since our last meeting. I had no idea that your hostility then was so final.'

Mary spoke up clearly and sharply:

'What else did you expect? After first wanting me to murder my child. And then making it clear that you had never even thought about marriage.'

Powerful words. Tom winced. The couple had reached the heart of the matter straightaway. In his defence Tom now came up with a plausible response, which had not been heard before:

'Mary, remember, while you were not known to be pregnant, I had no reason to think about marriage. Nor had you. But the fact that it was never in my thoughts did not mean that I was always going to rule it out if circumstances changed.'

There was a brief pause, while Mary took this in. Then, instead of dallying over the preliminary question of whether they *might* get married – airing the pros and cons – she chose to go for the jugular:

'Are you now asking me to marry you?'

Tom knew that he was cornered. At that moment in those circumstances he dare not say 'no'. If he had done so, that would have been the end of the conversation. Mary would have sprung up and left.

'Yes. If that's what you want.'

So Tom's 'yes' was qualified. 'But is it what *you* want, Tom?'

Tom had no choice but to say 'Yes'.

'So you love me?'

In Mary's eyes this was of course the crucial question. Last time Tom had said that love was 'elusive'. Would he say the same again?

'Oh, Mary. Maybe I do … I probably do … I find you very attractive. Isn't that enough?'

Mary coloured.

'So you still do not know. You're now accepting the idea of marriage. But why? You say it's for love, but only maybe. So are you really acting for the sake of the child, your child as much as mine? To make it legitimate. I doubt it. Or is it really all for yourself? To save your job. I cannot marry someone who …'

Mary had kept her cool just long enough to build up this damning sequence of argument. But now she burst into tears, dashed out of the room and down to the ladies' washroom.

Her father had been sitting in the History office and heard her rush out. He was surprised that the conversation had ended so quickly, and rightly feared the worst. He waited for Mary to come out of the washroom, which she did after about five minutes.

She was still distressed, but was now composed enough to talk to her father. They went back into Professor Grey's empty office. Tom Tongue had fled back to his own room.

'It's over, Dad. He doesn't love me. He tried to talk me into marriage, but he only wants to save his own skin, his job here.'

'I'm not surprised. I feared so. The man's a rogue. Still, there's no point in wringing our hands to no purpose. We must decide what to do next … what we as a family want in the long term. There are four of us now. And the university must settle what it should do, and we must say that marriage is finally ruled out. I think they'd still been hoping for marriage – they wanted it as a smokescreen.'

'Yes.'

'But we don't need to make any family decisions today. This afternoon we can hear from the Vice Chancellor what the university has in mind for itself. It will want to minimise the damage. We can try to help.'

Professor Grey of course ensured that Mary and her father had lunch with him in the refectory. Sitting together gave them all a chance to relax and to talk discursively. It showed Grey at his concerned best, clear-minded but gentle towards Mary.

'Mary, we'd better make it plain straightaway to the VC that marriage is definitely out. Otherwise even now he might begin by talking about that, since it's what he's hoped for. He must be told clearly that you've found Tom Tongue unacceptable, and that this fact has been finally confirmed today. You'll not want to go into details, but perhaps, Mary, you could simply say. "He does not love me". That would sound conclusive. The VC will not dare to enquire further.'

Mary simply smiled and said: 'Yes, that sounds right'.

Her father added pointedly: 'No quizzing of Mary.'

Andrew Grey made a brief phone call to the Dean to keep him in the picture. Then just before two-thirty he led Mary and her father to the Vice Chancellor's office. The Dean and Daniel Mellors followed them in. The Vice Chancellor welcomed Mary and her father smilingly, and spoke disarmingly.

'Welcome to you both. I say so with sincerity, although of course we all of us wish that this meeting had never been necessary.'

He paused while everyone sat down.

'Where to begin? I read Mr Parker's letter with alarm – both for you, Mary, and for the university. We have no choice but to sort things out as far as possible. I understand that you spoke again to Tom Tongue this morning. Has that led to any progress?'

The VC addressed his question half to Mary but half to the Dean. Guy Johnson, perceptive as ever, seized his chance finally to dismiss the marriage solution, which he and the VC had of course hoped for:

'I understand, Vice Chancellor, that this morning's meeting between Mary and Tom Tongue changed nothing. Marriage is ruled out.'

Mary saw her chance timidly to say her piece, as recommended by her Professor:

'He does not love me.'

The Vice Chancellor took the hint – no point in pursuing the personal dimension with Mary. He turned instead to her father:

'Mr Parker, your letter made it plain that you do not regard this unfortunate business as simply a family matter – you expect the university to take action against Tom Tongue. I'm inclined to agree. If the gutter press hear of this episode they'll have a field-day. We'll have to do something pre-emptive to minimise the damage to the good name of the university. Let me ask each of you in turn what you think such action might be … Mr Parker?'

Mary's father was taken slightly by surprise, but soon recovered.

'Er, thank you, Vice Chancellor. Well, yes. I think it's clear enough. I've no doubt that Tom Tongue deserves to be dismissed. No doubt at all. For the university's sake as well as Mary's. Could you ever trust such a man in the future? Sacrificing him will make it clear that this sort of thing is intolerable within the university. As much as to us, Mary's parents. Dismissal will not stop the newspapers, but at least it will make what they say a bit less damning.'

'Yes, I agree,' said the Dean. 'Not to dismiss him would prompt even worse publicity – charges that Blackchester was not interested in the moral welfare of its students. It's our legal obligation to those under twenty-one – *in loco parentis*'.

The Professor of English was of course closest to Tom Tongue. He might have spoken more in sorrow than in anger. But he didn't. 'There's no justification,' was all he said.

The Professor of History spoke last:

'There are matters of procedure to think about – dismissal or enforced resignation? Immediate or at an agreed date? But we need not trouble Mr Parker and Mary with these.'

The Vice Chancellor nodded.

'It looks as though we've come to a quick and decisive agreement as far as Tom Tongue is concerned. Mary's future plans are not really for this meeting. But Mary, you'll have to decide eventually whether you want to come back to the university, and when. We hope that you will come back.'

Mary smiled, less timidly this time.

'Thank you, Vice Chancellor.'

The Vice Chancellor offered his guests tea, but Mr Parker declined.

'We ought to get back home. I prefer to drive in as much daylight as possible.'

Mr Parker and Mary did not say anything of note in the car. They were mentally drained. But over the next few weeks and months the Parkers knew that they would have to plan for a summer baby.

(7)

Meanwhile, as Mary and her father drove away, the VC, Dean and two Professors were left in earnest conversation about ways and means. They had agreed that Tom Tongue must be removed from Blackchester; but how could his departure be best contrived?

The Vice Chancellor asked a key question: 'How many people on campus actually know about Mary's pregnancy?'

'Nobody apart from ourselves, so far as I know,' answered. Andrew Grey. 'She said at lunch that she had not even told her best friend. And she never went to the medical centre.'

The Vice Chancellor brightened. 'Excellent. Tell her to keep it that way. Keep the pregnancy in Sheffield. That way there's hope that the news will never leak out here. That the press will never hear of it.'

'In that case', added the Dean, 'Tom must not be "dismissed" – not in so many words. There must be no announcement to that effect. He must simply "resign" – but not "forthwith", for that too would attract notice. His name must simply appear among the usual list of resignations and appointments for next autumn.'

The Vice Chancellor agreed. 'Yes, let's call him in. He's waiting on campus. If we can get him to offer his resignation in the normal way we'll be moving in the right direction. Will he play ball?' The VC put this last question especially to the Professor of English.

'I think so. He must realise that he could never be comfortable here, even if the whole thing could be hushed up.'

The VC's secretary phoned Tom Tongue's office, and within ten minutes he was being questioned by the trio.

Tom looked subdued, and with good reason. If, after all, Mary had been persuaded into marriage, he knew that he would have been told so by now – probably by Mary herself. He knew that his job was on the line.

The VC spoke first:

'Dr Tongue, I think you know that we've just had an important meeting with the Parkers.'

'Yes.'

'We understand that marriage between you and Mary Parker has been flatly ruled out by Mary. Marriage would have limited the bad publicity for the university. But we are where we are, and we have been discussing what the university must do now.'

'Yes. I too have been thinking hard.'

'The university cannot ignore a sexual relationship between a lecturer and a student under twenty-one. Such students are *in statu pupillari*. You were in a position of trust and have abused that trust. What you have done is far too serious to be covered by a simple reprimand. You will have to leave the university. How can that best be achieved? Can it be done by mutual agreement? We hope so. Have you any suggestions?'

Tom noticed that the VC had cleverly avoided using the word 'dismissal'. And, for reasons of his own, Tom too wanted to keep it out of the conversation. In his own mind he had now realised that he must resign. It meant that both sides shared an interest in making his departure look as normal as possible. And Tom now said so.

'I hope we're both talking about my resignation. If we are, our discussion narrows down to how and when. That's how I see it.'

The quartet liked what they were hearing, and the Vice Chancellor spoke encouragingly:

'Go on, Dr Tongue.'

'I received just before Christmas a letter from a Canadian university. It asked if I would be interested in taking a post there. A visiting chair certainly, but possibly a permanent chair if I so preferred and by agreement. They wanted me to meet their Dean who will be in London next month. I've written back arranging to see him.'

The Professor of English now spoke for the first time.

'That sounds very interesting, Tom. It explains why I was quizzed about you by a Canadian Professor at a conference last autumn.'

The Vice Chancellor immediately realised how helpful Tom Tongue's new information might be:

'Well, Dr Tongue, what you say is very promising. It may be your way out. Your way out in two senses. We must trust so.'

The Dean added the vital gloss:

'It will mean that you simply resign in the normal way from next October. Do you accept that?'

'Yes. I do.'

Andrew Grey spoke for the first time to offer an important reminder:

'Mary tells me that no one in the university apart from ourselves knows about her pregnancy, not even her best friend. It's possible that the press will never know, if we play our cards right, and keep quiet.'

Tom responded: 'Good. Myself, I've told no one.' He smiled for the first time. 'We all want me to disappear quietly.'

The Vice Chancellor did not smile but summed up briskly:

'Well, this has turned out more hopeful than we had feared. You will of course let me know straightaway the result of your meeting with the Canadian. If he offers you the post, you will submit your resignation from Blackchester in the usual way. If there's no offer, we shall have to meet again.'

(8)

As soon as the new term began in January 1955 the Professor of History called in Joan Peters for a delicate chat:

'I gather Mary Parker is your friend. That's why I've asked to see you. You've no doubt heard that she's ill and will not be coming back this term. Have you heard why?'

'No. It's a bit odd. She was vague on the phone.'

'Well, I'm going to tell you in the strictest confidence that she is pregnant. I do so in the expectation that you will therefore dampen down all speculation by other students. I won't tell you who the father is. Only that if it got out it would be very damaging for the university, very damaging indeed. Best therefore for it not to be known even that she's pregnant.'

Joan's answer was knowing, but reassuring:

'I think I can guess who the father is. But of course I shall say nothing to anyone. If pressed, I'll invent something about a chronic illness.'

Tom Tongue duly met his Canadian Professor, and had a fruitful meeting. The Canadian was empowered to offer a visiting chair on the spot, and said that 'very probably' a permanent appointment could follow after a year.

This was of course not quite cast-iron, but Tom was conscious of his weak position with regard to Blackchester. In the last resort they would dismiss him, and then his career would be in ruins. Going to Canada was safe. It looked normal. He told himself that he might even have gone there anyhow.

However, Tom's resignation was not to be the end of the episode, for soon after Easter unexpected news came down from Sheffield – Mary Parker had suffered a sudden miscarriage at six months.

Physically, her young body soon got over the effects; but understandably, she took several weeks to come to terms with what had happened. Was it good news or was it bad news? Good perhaps that she was free again: certainly bad that a life had been lost. After all, she had firmly refused to have an abortion. She would never forget her child.

Mary eventually wrote to her Professor to tell him what had happened, and he replied very sympathetically:

'You must come back. You can make a new start. Put the past behind you, and get a good degree.'

Tom Tongue's resignation had already been announced, and when Grey told his three colleagues about Mary's changed situation, they all agreed that there could be no question of keeping Tom in post after all. He had broken the unwritten rules, and so could not stay.

As it happened, they need not have worried, for he never asked to stay. He knew that nothing had changed so far as the university was concerned.

Mary returned as a second-year student in October 1955. This time she was not tempted to choose an optional English course. This confirmed that it had been the man and not the subject which had attracted her a year earlier. Both teacher and pupil had paid a high price for her choice.

6

Coming and Going

(1)

Tom Tongue's departure meant that he would have to be replaced in October 1955 – not necessarily by a senior lecturer, but certainly by someone with teaching experience able to hold the interest of the much increased number of first-year 'Shakespeare to Shaw' students.

However, even before he knew about the pregnancy crisis, Daniel Mellors had begun to hatch other English staff demands.

'As the leading subject in the Faculty I think the time has come for us to appoint a second Professor. It will demonstrate to outsiders our high standing within the university world. We could also use it to indicate our breadth of interests. We could make it a new chair of American Literature.'

Mellors aired these ambitions first to the English board, where of course his colleagues all agreed enthusiastically. He next spoke to the Dean:

'I hope I'm pushing at an open door, Guy. It seems obvious that expansion means more than numbers. It means range and reputation.'

The Dean was inclined to agree; and he knew that the other subjects in the Faculty must accept such an expansion, even including those less popular subjects which could not expect many (if any) new posts themselves. His own subject, Classics, was one of these. Characteristically, he wanted progress without confrontation:

'Let's have an informal meeting of Professors over dinner at my house to think about the future shape of the Faculty.' Guy Johnson hoped that a good meal with good wine would produce a more relaxed atmosphere than a meeting round a table in his office.

The Dean waited until Tom Tongue had confirmed in writing that he was going to Canada. He then fixed the dinner for just a week later. Each of the Professors realised that Tom's resignation conveniently opened up the whole question of future posts. Would there be any new posts for them, including even chairs? The Professors of English and History were determined that there must indeed soon be new chairs for themselves.

The Dean started with Tom Tongue:

'The simplest move would be to appoint another senior lecturer in Tom's place. He must certainly be replaced at some level. But I sense that several of you want to go further than that, and I agree. Now is the time to think several years ahead. I know that you, Daniel, have some bold thoughts.'

'Yes, Guy. We're the fastest-growing subject in the Faculty. We'll need several new posts. Teaching range is important in attracting student numbers. At the top of my requests I would place the appointment of a second Professor. That would give us extra status both within the university and outside. We could use the appointment to add to our range by making it a chair in American Literature. That is of course a big and popular subject. The schools would like it.'

This was the first Andrew Grey had heard of a second chair for English, although he recalled that Mellors had hinted to him during the Tom Tongue crisis that he wanted more than a simple replacement for the vacancy.

Grey reacted fast and to good purpose. He was ready enough to accept the idea of a second chair for English so long as it could be used to extract more than one new post for History, including a chair. He decided that the clever thing to do was to jump enthusiastically on the Mellors bandwagon.

'Yes, I think the university now needs second chairs in both English and History. I am of course myself a British History specialist. We must not appear myopic. We need a chair in European History.'

The Dean was encouraging:

'Yes, I recognise the argument. We must be seen to link ourselves with both America and Europe.'

He turned to the Professor of French. 'I take it French would like more coverage of Europe and America? It would encourage joint-degree packages.'

The Professor of French, eager to find extra students, accepted the bait:

'We could certainly then offer some worthwhile packages in French and History or French and English.'

Mellors naturally liked the way the conversation was going. But he also wanted more lectureships.

'Tom Tongue was of course a senior lecturer at the top of the range. We do not need to replace him at that level. We could appoint a lecturer – young but with some experience. And then put the money towards the assistant lectureship which Dick Rogers currently occupies. His tenure ends in the autumn. I suggest we keep him by giving him a lectureship at the bottom of the scale. He has proved very lively as a teacher, and has turned out to be a good interviewer when we had to press him into service because of the large number of applicants.'

Mellors was cleverly mixing boldness with moderation. His colleagues found it difficult to count up the number and cost of his demands. The Professors in the smaller subjects wanted reassurance that the costs of English expansion would not rule them out entirely for the future. By contrast, the Professor of History decided to assume that the expansion of English, far from ruling History out, would rule it in:

'I could go along with what Daniel is wanting because it matches what we also need in History. Early modern history is very popular with our students, and we need extra help there. We could make that one lectureship, but I would prefer instead two very junior assistant lectureships, making the second one a medievalist. We have only a single medievalist at present.'

This expansionist line was not merely adroit in itself: it was well timed. By arguing for it at that moment, with Mellors exposed, Grey was blandly assuming that the Professor of English would be sympathetic to History's requests. Grey was right. Mellors responded supportively, with no more taunts against History.

'All this sounds reasonable to me. English and History have the future of the Faculty in their hands. We must recognise that.'

Here was an unholy alliance but a powerful one. Afterwards, the conversation ran on easily enough during the meal. The assumption was that English and History would get the approval of Faculty Board and Senate.

The Dean had his own reasons for being a forceful advocate.

'I have good Faculty grounds for backing you both. Politically we must be demanding, even insistent, at Senate. Social Science is also asking for new posts this autumn. Yet their student numbers are growing much less quickly than ours. They're talking about their need for seed-corn to attract numbers – whatever that's supposed to mean. Lecturers in this-and-that to look good in the prospectus!'

The dinner guests smiled. But the Dean continued his warning about the Social Scientists:

'We must watch them. If they don't attract significantly increased student numbers in the near future they must not be allowed to ask for yet more staff. On the other hand, we can insist upon still more if English and History continue to grow. I only wish we could attract more modern language students. Perhaps next year French should try the seed-corn argument. Social Science could not dismiss it as bogus, having used it itself.'

(2)

We have mentioned Richard Corke only occasionally, even though he was the most popular lecturer in the History department. Aged thirty, he was still young enough to provide a useful link with the students. He often gave them coffee, and he had Sunday lunch parties at his flat in town. His colleagues knew that if they needed to know 'what the students think' it was always worth asking Richard. He was a bachelor, which gave him time and freedom. Why had he not married, or apparently had a girlfriend? Discreet questions had begun to be asked about his sexual orientation, but all very quietly.

Then one Monday morning, just before the end of the winter term in March 1955, he failed to turn up to give a lecture. And in the afternoon he failed to give a seminar. Where was he? Students told the departmental secretary about his absences. She found that his office was locked. She rang his home address, but got no reply. Perhaps he had been away over the weekend, and his train had been delayed. But when he failed to show up for the seminar she decided that she must tell Professor Grey.

He expressed only mild concern:

'There's probably a simple explanation.'

However, when Richard Corke failed to appear on the Tuesday morning they began to wonder. Corke lived in a flat only just off campus, so Grey decided to walk down there. There were four flats in the Victorian house, with Corke's the first one on the ground floor as you went in. Grey rang the bell firmly twice, but got no reply. He went upstairs to another flat, and found the woman occupant in.

'No, I've not seen or heard him for several days. I usually do see him coming or going.'

Andrew Grey was becoming worried. What to do? He decided to wait one more day; but when there was still no sign of his colleague on the Wednesday morning he concluded that the university must act. He phoned the police, and arranged for a forced entry.

Corke's body was found in his bath, which was full of water. He had cut his wrists and bled to death. A classic suicide.

Staff and students, both in the History department and more widely within the university, were of course shocked. How could this have happened? He was so outgoing.

There was no explanatory suicide note. What about friends? It emerged that although Corke was well known and popular in general, he had no particular friend who knew his inner thoughts. Here perhaps was a clue. Although he was good with people in general, and socialised readily enough, he never seemed go to the further stage of being close with anyone in particular, male or female.

Evidence at the inquest revealed this background, which was entirely unexpected. The other historians felt guilty. Clearly, they had missed something about their colleague, for they now realised that his popularity had been misleading. They talked together, but with little confidence until Peter Price, the medievalist and the most detached of the historians, came up with an explanation. Price was glad to do so, for he had always been jealous of Corke's popularity. Price dared to suggest that Corke might have been a closet homosexual:

'Maybe he found himself attracted to young men, and had

to resist it. He didn't want any particular woman, and yet he couldn't have any particular man. In the end he snapped.'

But no one knew the reality. There had been a male student who, by chance, Corke had taught in each of the student's three years. The young man in question – with classical good looks: slim, blonde-haired, rosy-cheeked, soft-skinned – had no idea that he was physically attractive to Richard Corke. If he had understood the situation he would surely have decided at the start of his third year not to take Corke's special subject, for this brought them together in weekly one-to-one tutorials to discuss essays. Although Corke never revealed his feelings to the student, these repeated encounters had left him increasingly in mental turmoil. He found himself looking forward to each meeting and yet appalled that he was doing so. One weekend it all became too much for him to bear any longer. He went into his bathroom and filled the bath with hot water …

The student never knew why his tutor had killed himself. And the History staff were left equally ignorant about the young man's unwitting central role. For everyone, the effect was clear enough, and yet the underlying cause was undiscoverable by anyone.

So the History staff could do no more than speculate in general terms. And when Professor Grey was told of Price's (correct but now unprovable) interpretation of what had happened, he tried to be tersely dismissive, both for Corke's sake and for the department's:

'Do you really think so?'

Yet Grey had to accept in his own mind that this explanation could well be right, even if he admitted so only to the Dean. Grey liked to think that he ran a happy ship; yet this unexpected revelation suggested otherwise. In the absence of a suicide note, the inquest added to the uncertainty by recording an open verdict.

The English department – whose image within the

university had been damaged by the 'bite' episode – was glad to notice flippantly that History had obviously been housing a troubled soul:

'Sad of course. Our Tom's taking himself off to Canada. But where's Richard Corke gone?'

(3)

Advertisements for chairs in History and English, and for various lectureships, duly appeared just after Easter 1955. These now included Corke's vacant lectureship as a last-minute addition. The hope was that many junior posts could be filled by October, although it was realised that some senior people interested in the chairs might not be available so quickly.

Andrew Grey gave particular attention to applications for the Professorship in Modern European History. He mentioned the vacancy when attending meetings at the Historical Association and Royal Historical Society. There was known to be a shortage of good Europeanists, and consequently the field of applicants was not especially strong. But five were called for interview. Professor Medlicott, President of the Historical Association, agreed to serve as an outside assessor, along with Professor George Potter from Sheffield University.

All this was entirely normal – except in one regard. One of the candidates was the brother of the Professor of English!

The application from Dr. Michael Mellors arrived on the very last possible day. Andrew Grey had been checking the post as it came in. Some candidates were too old, and some too young. Their publication record was patchy, with only a few having made really significant contributions to European history. Then came the Michael Mellors application.

He was clearly a good candidate – a senior lecturer at Leeds University, author of a major study of the French Revolution. He had wide teaching experience, not least in the United States, where he had spent a year. His three referees confirmed all this, although none of them said much about his personality.

When Andrew Grey first saw the name 'Michael Mellors' his hand froze. Was this a relative of the Professor of English? The surname was uncommon. Heaven help us! Grey decided that he would have to check. He picked up the phone and rang the Professor of English.

'Daniel. Andrew Grey here. We're going through the applications for the chair of History. One in particular has caught my eye. It's from a 'Michael Mellors' at Leeds. Do you know anything about this man?'

'Oh, yes. He's my brother. Five years older than me.' Daniel Mellors said this almost matter-of-factly; but he must have known that the news would shake his great rival.

Andrew Grey swallowed hard. He really needed time to think about such a bombshell, but he managed to come up with one pertinent question:

'Did you know about this?'

'Oh, yes. He came here a few weeks ago and had a look round. He liked the place.'

'What do you think?'

'Oh, it's not really for me to comment upon his qualifications.'

This was a fair answer; yet Grey was not asking about Mellors's qualifications but about the wisdom of appointing a colleague's brother in such circumstances, whatever his academic merits.

Grey realised that he would have to discuss this unexpected problem with the Dean and others before they reached the stage of calling for interview.

'What do we do, Guy? Is he ruled out almost automatically? Or do we take no notice at all of the family connection? No notice at any stage. In other words, are we no more and no less likely to appoint a second Mellors?'

'All good questions, Andrew. This is a tester. It would of course be solved if we could say that he is not strong enough academically, and so could rule him out without interview. But from what you say he's a good candidate, well qualified for interview.'

'Yes.'

'You'd better contact the assessors. Send them copies of his application, with a covering letter explaining that he's the brother of the Professor of English. Then phone each of them for a discussion.'

'I'll do that.'

'My guess is that they'll say that he cannot be ruled out automatically. That we ought to interview him. It may be that we'll then prefer someone else. If so, the problem eventually fades away.'

Andrew Grey was hoping to say nothing more about the matter to the Professor of English; but the latter phoned, and Grey had to reveal that Michael Mellors was going to be called for interview.

The English Professor should have left it at that, but he didn't. He knowingly stirred the pot by adding mischievously, 'I trust his relationship to me is not going to be regarded as a disqualification.'

Grey decided that the best way to stifle this probing comment was to be flippant:

'Not at all. We may well decide that we want more of you!'

The interviews for the chair of Modern European History all took place on the same day towards the end of May 1955. The five selected candidates were each given an hour, and told that they might be called again for a further interview. Two were selected. One was John Richards from Liverpool University: the other was Michael Mellors from Leeds.

At interview, these two had been found to be much the strongest candidates. They reappeared a week later. After further questioning, it was agreed that Mellors did not reveal himself so readily as Richards. Was there something guarded about him? In the end the personality point gave Richards the edge. A letter was sent to him offering him the chair 'from a date to be arranged'.

So the brother problem had been averted – or so it seemed for a few days.

But when no letter or phone-call of speedy acceptance came back from Richards in Liverpool fears began to surface. Why the delay? In the end the Dean agreed that Andrew Grey should phone Liverpool. What he then discovered was unexpected. It emerged that Richards was in the process of accepting the offer of a chair from another more prestigious university – he had been running Blackchester and Bristol in tandem!

When told about this, the Blackchester interviewers were angry; but there was nothing that they could do about it. Such duplicity was bad enough. Worse still – given that Michael Mellors was the only other candidate still in the running – they were left to face 'the brother of Mellors question' after all. Should he therefore now be offered the chair? If not, why not?

Andrew Grey discussed the new Mellors problem informally with his History colleagues. Many cups of tea and coffee were drunk uneasily. The questions and implications were various. Did they think that to have the brother of the Professor of English among them would be like having a spy in the camp? Would they ever again feel free to say rude things about English in general and about Daniel Mellors in particular? Their answer was 'no' – at least not in the presence of his brother. Did such new restraint matter? Would it affect the quality of History teaching and planning at Blackchester?

'Perhaps not,' said Adam Thwaite, the shrewd senior lecturer, who had been one of the interviewing panel, 'but it would affect the social tone of the department. We would certainly feel uneasy together at first, perhaps unfairly. Things might calm down after a bit if Michael Mellors showed himself to be a model personality – aware of the problem and good-humoured, saying frankly that he was his own man and confirming this by his actions.'

The Professor of History repeated these wise thoughts to the Dean, who agreed with their drift.

'Well, Andrew, can we be confident that Michael Mellors would act in such a way? We thought he was rather guarded at interview. We just don't know. We would be taking a risk. Should we do so? If things went wrong it would shatter the morale of your department for a long time. The university would lose as well as the historians.'

The last word rested with the Dean. No one could be appointed to the Faculty if he disapproved. He thought it prudent to bring the VC into the picture. For once, Roger Walker avoided the usual Vice Chancellorial evasion when faced with a testing question:

'I understand your difficulty, Guy. Ought anyone's brother to have applied? How vital is it to make this appointment? Perhaps you should wait a year, and then try again. Merely my thoughts. I'm not exercising any veto.'

Veto or not, this conversation proved conclusive. The Dean went back to Andrew Grey and they agreed that they could not run the risk of appointing Michael Mellors. They noted that, when pressed, no one had said that they should. The university could try again next year – perhaps with a chair not in European but in American History.

Michael Mellors was duly informed of the university's 'regret' in a letter. A final sentence added that 'the university has decided not to make an appointment for the present'. This last was merely for information, and need not have been said. But more was to be heard about it.

(4)

Daniel Mellors had been following events from a distance, and had gathered that there were two candidates at the last, his brother and a man from Liverpool. The latter had been preferred, but had turned it down. This refusal meant, so Daniel Mellors now began to assume, that his brother would be quickly offered the chair.

When he heard that this was not the case, and that the historians were agonising, he became angry. He went to the Dean.

'Why the delay, Guy? You have two candidates thought worthy of the chair. One withdraws, so you offer it to the other. It seems obvious. What are you waiting for?'

The Dean felt uncomfortable, but had an answer.

'We never actually said whether, if the Liverpool man turned us down, we would automatically make an offer to your brother. The implication was that we would think about it. That's what we are now doing.'

'"Implication" is a very wobbly word, Guy. I suspect that the delay is not on academic grounds at all, and is entirely to do with the fact that Michael is my brother.'

Guy Johnson could only offer a holding answer:

'Wait and see, Daniel. Nothing is finalised.'

'Yes, I will wait. But I reserve my position. I may have to go to a higher level. The VC, or even Lord Ongar.'

Ongar was the Chairman of Council, the ultimate governing body of the university. Its chairman was always an outsider of wide experience who wielded considerable authority.

The Dean did not immediately reveal to the Professor of History that Daniel Mellors was threatening trouble. No use stoking up the fires of History/English tension. If Michael Mellors were eventually to be given the chair, even if after some delay, no need for History to know about these threats.

But when the decision had been made not to offer him the appointment, Guy Johnson had no choice but to reveal to the interviewing panel that the Professor of English was likely to speak out.

'He has threatened to go to the Vice Chancellor and beyond. He claims that we had committed ourselves to offer the chair to his brother if Richards refused.'

The Professor of History responded with what became the formal explanation.

'Yet we never said so definitely, Guy. Mellors was our second choice, if a choice had to be made, *but not an automatic choice.* We have thought about it again, and have decided not to make an offer at all. It's all perfectly reasonable and defensible.'

The Dean nodded. 'Yes, to us maybe. But we must be careful not to say that we changed our minds, since that implies we had originally intended to make an offer to Michael Mellors, if need be. We must say that our minds were never finally made up with regard to him, even though he was second on our list. Such uncertainty did not really matter while we thought our first choice would accept.'

The Professor of English now wrote to the Vice Chancellor requesting an interview. The letter outlined what Daniel Mellors regarded as the basic questions – 'Why was my brother not made an offer, given that he was second on the list? Was this in any way to do with the fact that he is my brother? If so, was this penalisation reasonable?'

In his letter Daniel Mellors did not add that he might want these questions to be tested at law; but he did say so verbally when he met the VC.

The threat of going to law alarmed the VC most of all. Whatever the outcome, he knew that such publicity would damage the drive to sell the university as an active but calm seat of learning. This would apply even if Blackchester eventually won any legal case. The VC tried to explain this damaging consequence to Daniel Mellors, but Mellors refused to be frightened:

'You may be right about the publicity. But I have to seek justice for my brother. I'm not convinced that justice has been done. I shall take legal advice.'

The Vice Chancellor decided that he had better do the same, but not formally. He had a friend who was a QC, and decided to talk to him. This friend expressed concern. He warned that if anything in writing had suggested or even implied that Michael Mellors was to be made an offer in the event of Richards refusing, then Blackchester needed to be careful. The university would only be in the clear if the interviewing panel had done two things, preferably in one formal vote which linked the two. It needed, first, to admit that its original inclination had indeed been to make an offer to Mellors if Richards declined; and second it needed explicitly to have abandoned any such intention.

None of this had been done. There had been much informal time-wasting discussion, face-to-face and over the phone. Attention had been diverted into persuading one another that the obligation to make an offer had never been absolutely firm. Yet in law it could be argued that the original intention had been clear enough. What was needed was a clear change of mind by the interviewing panel with regard to Michael Mellors.

The two outside assessors had eventually agreed to the rejection of Mellors, but they had done so only over the phone. The Vice Chancellor now insisted that the panel reconvene. He would meet them himself to explain what was needed. The assessors were busy men, but they agreed to return at short notice one Sunday. They were given a good lunch, and afterwards a formal motion was unanimously agreed: 'The panel recommends unanimously that no offer be made to the remaining candidate, and that the search for a Professor of Modern History be postponed for the present.'

There was some discussion about whether they should name Michael Mellors. Candidates for academic posts were usually given anonymity outside, and in the end this convention was maintained.

In the event, it scarcely mattered, for the Professor of English had begun to talk on campus loud and long in support of his brother. The Vice Chancellor sent him a copy of the panel's motion in the hope that it would stifle his complaints. But in response, far from quietening down, Daniel Mellors sought to raise the matter both at Faculty Board and at Senate.

Faculty Board came first. Mellors sent the Dean a formal written enquiry, which sounded innocuous but wasn't:

'Why has there been no appointment to the chair of Modern History advertised some time ago?'

The Dean refused to respond.

'You know as well as I do, Daniel, that all discussions at interviewing panels are confidential. My answer at the board would have to be dismissive, simply saying that no available candidate had been up to standard. I would not be willing to discuss how that decision had been arrived at.'

'I suspect that you ruled out one appointable candidate for no other reason than that he was my brother.'

'No, Daniel, we might have appointed him even though he was your brother. I'm not willing to say more than that.'

This answer was true enough, but it was of course incomplete, and it left Daniel Mellors baffled. He stormed out of the Dean's office.

He did even less well with the Vice Chancellor, who flatly refused to put any question about the unfilled chair on the Senate agenda:

'I hope you will concentrate upon filling your new chair of American Literature.'

The Professor of English knew that he had now exhausted all lines of internal enquiry. Did he really want to consider taking the university to law? He spoke to his friend, the Professor of French, about this, but received no encouragement. Quite the contrary:

'I see why you're wanting to persist, Daniel. You suspect Faculty dirty linen. But for that very reason we must not wash it. We would all suffer. That is point one. And suppose you won, and your brother did come here. After such a rumpus how would he fit in? Into the Faculty in general and into History in particular? He would be unloved.'

This last point was what finally persuaded Daniel Mellors to give up. Concern for his brother still influenced him; but now his brotherly love shifted from being urgently positive to being sadly negative. He concluded that Michael would not be happy at Blackchester.

And who did the Professor of English blame for all this?

'That tricky blighter Andrew Grey. I don't know all the details; but I'm sure he had no intention of ever accepting my brother as a colleague!'

Perhaps Mellors was right. But if so, Grey had never entirely revealed himself – not to his colleagues, nor to his wife, and perhaps not even to himself.

(5)

In the past Tom Tongue would have been consulted by Daniel Mellors about what was happening. But not now. Recent events had left the Professor of English on his own.

Fortunately, only Daniel and Tom himself among the English staff knew why Tom was going; and only Joan Peters among the students. So he was given a good send-off on the last day of term – a lively party in Wells hall, with food, drink, music and dancing. Many expressed genuine regret at Tom's going. He delivered a light-hearted farewell speech, which ranged widely but gave nothing away:

'In going, I wish Blackchester well. It's a new university

which deserves to succeed. But I'm doing even better in terms of newness, for I'm going to a whole new world.'

And only a few noticed that – because of the 'bite' business – none of the History staff attended.

7

Brotherly Love?

(1)

A new academic year began in October 1955, and with it a new label for its graduates: all degrees conferred by the university would now be 'Blackchester' degrees.

Andrew Grey decided to talk about this to his students. At the beginning of term he called a meeting of all three years in the Arts lecture theatre.

'I thought I would bring you all together because this is a special moment. From now on you are all candidates for "Blackchester" degrees. The London umbrella has gone. This makes it especially important that you do well. Important as always for each of you, but also extra-important for the department and the university. We want it to become known that our History graduates are of above-average quality – above-average in intellect regardless of whether or not they choose to use their history after graduation as school teachers or the like. You have a novel responsibility.'

The students quite liked to be told that they were special. One of them in the audience was Mary Parker, who had returned to the second-year. Her friends from the past were of course now third-years. These included Joan Peters. When they first met, Mary did not know whether to reveal the truth about her 'illness' or not. Fortunately, Joan recognised her difficulty, and decided that it would be best to explain that Professor Grey had spoken to her.

'He did not say who the father was. But I told him that I could guess. I assume it was Tom Tongue.'

'Yes.'

'Right. Well, we needn't talk about it ever again. You have a new life to start.'

Mary found that she needed Joan's sensible support in those first few weeks. During the course of the previous academic year she had been forced to switch uncomfortably from being a student to being a prospective mother, and now she had to switch back again. During that same year she might have become not only a mother but also a wife. Now it had all faded.

Inevitably she was not the same person as the girl who had started that second-year of teaching twelve months previously. At first, she had let her mind wander in lectures, especially if the lecturers were not as good as Tom Tongue. She found herself making comparisons. Then she would check herself. She would remind herself that Tom was not a good model: he had used her.

At first, she did not become close to any other second-year students, for they already had their friends from the previous year. So she began to feel lonely. Had she been wise to come back?

But then things changed. On several occasions in succession, she chanced to sit beside the same man. He was obviously the shy type, which explained why he was still 'available'. Mary found herself taking pity on him. One morning, when the lecturer was late, she started talking to her neighbour with increasing freeness. Afterwards she found herself saying: 'Shall we go for a coffee?'

He looked surprised but pleased. His name was Peter Proudfoot.

It emerged that they had something in common, and this

helped to bring them together. They discovered that they both came from Sheffield, and lived in adjacent suburbs. They agreed that it was underrated as a city, and was much more than just a steel-making town. Mary noticed how they shared a mild version of the same Yorkshire accent, and she found this reassuring.

So Mary and Peter were becoming good for one another. Mary settled into her History courses, while Peter became more outgoing and animated, even if his appearance remained unprepossessing. He had straight dark hair, a pale, slightly spotty face coupled with a serious expression, and his wire glasses were basic. All very academic. Last year, Mary would have scarcely looked at him.

His room was in Wells, and Mary started to go to the refectory expecting to find him in the meal queue. They went to the cinema in town several times. Eventually, and hesitantly, he took hold of Mary's hand, and she did not object. Yet they never went to Mary's room – or his. After the cinema they said goodbye at her hall's entrance. Finally, on the fifth occasion he pecked her farewell on the cheek.

Would he invite her to the Liberal Christmas ball? He did not dance; but he began to wonder if he should learn. This was a daring thought by his standards. Eventually, he plucked up courage:

'Did you go to last year's dance, Mary?'

She did indeed go – with Tom Tongue, although they did not arrive together. And Tom had covered his tracks by dancing also with lots of other students. But Mary could not reveal any of this. So she had to say 'no'.

'Would you like to go?'

'Are you inviting me?'

'Yes.'

'All right. I didn't know you were a dancer.'

'I'm not. I'll have to learn.'

This was hardly a romantic invitation. But it served.

Obviously they needed to practice. But where? Their need for private space led Mary to break down the barrier:

'Come to my room this evening, C12. I've got a few records we can try dancing to.'

In fact, like most contemporary teenagers, she was a keen record collector.

So Peter started to come to her room for practice. She made coffee. She did not have a sofa, so there was no temptation to sit together as there had been with Tom Tongue. It was the bed or fairly hard chairs – and they were a long way from being tempted by the bed. Nevertheless, Mary felt it strange to be with someone so inexperienced – in fact with a student with no experience of the opposite sex at all. What a contrast to Tom Tongue!

She smiled about this to herself, but it did not put her off. Peter was an innocent, but so be it. Underneath, she decided that he was 'nice'. Of course, she said nothing to him about her pregnancy, only that she had been 'ill'.

'Did you have a girlfriend last year, Peter? You never mention anyone.'

Peter looked uncomfortable, but spoke up in self-defence.

'No. I worked hard. I won the first-year prize.'

'Oh, congratulations. I hope I'm not too much of a distraction.'

Peter improvised a surprisingly mature answer. 'No. If I'd gone on like that I'd have become a first-class bore. Mind you, I still hope to get a first.'

Peter was fortunate in that he did not need much sleep. After an evening with Mary, he did not go straight to bed, but spent a couple of hours reading or writing essays. When he woke about seven o'clock, he read for an hour before breakfast. This dedication, plus his natural intelligence, ensured that he remained on course for a first.

Winning the first-year prize meant that he was particularly noticed by the History staff. His tutor was Adam Thwaite, who was pleased to find that during the autumn term Peter seemed to have become a warmer personality. Thwaite, who took over as Mary's tutor in place of Richard Corke, had noticed Peter in Mary's company. He mentioned this to Professor Grey:

'I know you're keeping a particular eye on Mary Parker, Andrew. I've seen her several times in the company of another of my tutees, Peter Proudfoot, the man who won the first-year prize. I saw them together at the cinema. Last year Peter was a dull dog, clever but dull: this year he's better.'

'And you attribute this to Mary?'

'It seems likely.'

'Well. Perhaps it will help her to settle down. Playing a mother figure, if that's what she's doing. Just so long as she doesn't become pregnant again.'

Adam Thwaite nodded. 'That goes without saying. But perhaps I'd better say it!'

He had of course spoken to Mary as her tutor at the beginning of term, but he thought it wise to call her in again after a fortnight, and again a month later. At this third meeting he thought it prudent to mention Peter.

'I think you know another of my tutees, Peter Proudfoot.'

'Yes.'

'I mention him for two reasons. Last year he was bright but lonely. This year he seems to be warmer. Is that because of your influence?'

'Maybe. We've got to know one another this term.'

'I welcome it for both your sakes. You must not be put off by what happened to you with Tom Tongue. You have the rest of your life in front of you.'

'Yes. He's quite a contrast. I suppose I mother him a bit.'

'That brings me to my second point. I have to say it for your sake. Whatever you do, don't get pregnant again.'

Mary looked shocked at the very thought.

'We're a long way from that.'

Adam Thwaite smiled supportively. Yet he couldn't help thinking that it was often the dismissive students who got caught.

(2)

The Professor of English was still restless. He had not forgiven the historians over the rejection of his brother. He remained convinced that it had happened not for sound academic reasons but because Michael Mellors was his brother. That was of course correct; but in a way which the English Professor was never told and never worked out for himself. Michael Mellors was rejected not for being a brother, but for being a brother whose personality had been found to be doubtful in such sensitive circumstances. Of course, the Professor of English would not have been calmed by any such full explanation even if he had been given one.

There was no similar tension over the appointment of a new Professor of American Literature, who had joined the university in October 1955. He was Geoffrey Boswell, a genial forty-year old bachelor, who seemed likely to fit well into the Faculty, if the historians would let him. Andrew Grey was hopeful.

'He seems pleasant. If he doesn't fall too much under the thumb of Daniel Mellors we might be able to cultivate him. We might turn the tables – if not exactly a spy in the English camp, at least a sympathiser.'

So the historians made a point of being nice to Geoffrey Boswell. Grey gave a dinner-party at his home for the newcomer, to which all the historians and their wives were invited. This was a special occasion, for Mrs Grey had never before given pride of place at her table to an English Professor. Daniel Mellors – who was occasionally invited when it became unavoidable – was not invited this time. The historians wanted the new man to themselves. The party went well, and ran late. Jennifer Grey seemed to get on particularly well with the new Professor.

Both English and History were busy absorbing their increased numbers of first-year students, and also their new lecturers. There were two new assistant lecturers in History, one eighteenth-century specialist and one medievalist. Both were young with little experience; but if they settled they could hope eventually to become full lecturers. Tanya Jenkins, who was now beginning her third year as an assistant lecturer, noticed this development. She had been warned on appointment that her own assistant lectureship was for three years only, and would not become a full lectureship. She had been told that the department liked to have new blood each time. Such had been the old attitude. But did this cut-off still apply?

Tanya felt that she had a double claim to stay on. Her lecturing in 'Shakespeare to Shaw' was important in launching the new first-year course smoothly, and her three lectures on Shakespeare and Milton had gone well. Also she had suffered in the 'bite' business – even though she did not know that her discomfort at the hands of Tom Tongue had been followed by his much worse misbehaviour in the case of Mary Parker. She had been shaken, and was glad when he took himself off to Canada.

Tanya decided to ask Professor Grey about her prospects at Blackchester.

'Andrew, I've been wondering about my future. This is the beginning of my final year here, if I've got to go after three years. Is that still the case?'

'Oh, I don't think anyone's been thinking about that.'

'Maybe not, but I need to. I notice that these new assistant lectureships are not time-limited.'

'Your type of post was set up just after the war, when expansion was still very slow. It was a way of injecting new blood into the department every three years. These recent posts are of course part of the new expansion plan.'

'I see all that. But I like it here and want to stay. If I have to go, I need to start planning soon, applying for jobs elsewhere. As you know, I've given some important lectures to the first-years. I think they went well. And of course there was the "bite" business. I was glad to have the support of the historians over that.'

'Yes. I think we can claim to have made the best of a bad job there. You handled yourself well. That must recommend you. But technically the post is fixed at three years. I'll talk to the Dean.'

The Dean was not immediately encouraging.

'I like Tanya. Probably we can do something. But let's wait a while until we know more about the UGC's intentions in the medium-term. The VC expects to hear more soon.'

So Tanya had no choice but to be patient. She had of course been pleased that her former boyfriend, Dick Rogers, who had held the equivalent assistant lectureship in English, had been kept on after three years and given a full lectureship.

They now met only casually in the common room. In return for being retained and promoted, Dick had become a Daniel Mellors loyalist. This meant that he was now permanently suspicious of the historians. When Tanya first congratulated him on his promotion he had commented upon her similar situation.

'Are you hoping for the same, Tanya? I shouldn't put all your eggs in that basket if I were you. It will depend upon Andrew Grey, and he's a tricky character. Daniel's been filling me in there.'

If by 'tricky' his English critics meant 'forward-thinking for History', Andrew Grey was certainly guilty. His first drive to attract extra students for the autumn of 1955 had been a success; but he realised that his department must keep up the publicity. All his lecturers were now giving talks to branches of the Historical Association, which spread the Blackchester name wide. And he himself had settled to give a half-hour talk on the BBC's Third Programme. It had the intriguing title: 'Men Who Never Became Prime Minister, and Why'. He hoped that such a title would attract more listeners than usually tuned in to such a highbrow channel. He was busy collecting colourful material on the likes of Joseph and Austen Chamberlain, father and son. He would certainly be quoting the remark made by a fellow politician that 'Austen always played the game, and he always lost it.'

But Grey realised that the attractive Blackchester campus needed to become much better known, visited by many more schoolteachers. And he contrived to take a notable step in such a direction by arranging a summer school for the Historical Association. It was to be held in August 1956, and housed in Wells hall of residence. From the start of the year he was busy planning the event. It was to have a hundred participants (mostly teachers) and ten course tutors. Eight tutors were to come from other universities, which was a tacit indication that Blackchester was now recognised as a significant centre for History.

Grey drew the attention of Faculty Board to this forthcoming event, pointing out its publicity value:

'A hundred keen types will be coming for the teaching, which is pleasing, while thousands more will read the publicity literature, which is also good. It reminds them of our History department.'

Grey was entitled to boast about all this, but he could not resist also taking an unwise swipe at English:

'I hope English will follow in our footsteps. We want the whole Faculty to be strong.'

The Professor of English rose readily to Grey's challenge:

'We may organise some future event for outsiders. But student numbers are what count most. We expect to grow yet further – not sixty as this year but sixty-five next October. What will History manage?'

This put Grey on the spot, for it looked as if History would do well to repeat next year its present intake of fifty.

'Too soon to say. But of course our summer-school publicity will bear fruit for the long-term. We must make sure the accommodation and food is up to a high standard – no skimping by the hall management.' Food rationing had recently ended, and Grey emphasised that wartime 'austerity' could no longer be tolerated at Blackchester. There was a new level of expectation.

With perfect timing, the Professor of English now dropped an unexpected bombshell. His brother had phoned him the previous evening with some striking news, which Daniel Mellors made the more effective by revealing in as few words as possible:

'Feed them up by all means. But you have no second Professor to offer a course. My brother rang me up last night to say that he had just been appointed to a chair at Manchester.'

Daniel Mellors drew no conclusions from this sudden revelation. He didn't need to. His brother had been rejected by Blackchester, the newest university, only to be welcomed by one of the oldest. The Dean and the Professor of History both looked uncomfortable. The Dean could only say weakly: 'Thank you for that good news, Daniel. I'm sure we all wish him well.'

(3)

The first Blackchester annual degree ceremony was now coming into prospect. It was fixed to be held on Saturday 7 July 1956. The public orator was to be Daniel Mellors, and he planned to wax eloquent in his speech, boasting not least about his own subject. Unfortunately, Blackchester did not yet possess a hall befitting such an occasion. The ceremony would perforce have to be held in Cavell's dining-hall, the largest available space.

However, at the start of 1956 the Vice Chancellor had launched an appeal for funds to build a separate new building, which would house degree ceremonies and public events. He had hinted that if a sufficiently generous benefactor were to be found, the hall could be named after him. However, the Professor of English hoped for a more significant name, preferably literary.

'Joe Bloggs Hall would lack distinction. How about Bernard Shaw or T.S. Eliot?'

In truth, Mellors was getting ahead of himself. The appeal rumbled on month by month with only moderate success, meaning that it would be several years before anything could be built. And unsurprisingly, the Professor of History was dismissive: 'I suppose we must be thankful that he does not want it to be named after his brother!'

The Dean heard about this quip, and decided to call Mellors and Grey together in order to urge them to stop sniping at one another:

'Competition is fair enough, but you need always to remember that you are pulling the same Faculty chariot.'

Andrew Grey smiled disingenuously.

'I hope I do.'

Daniel Mellors did not smile. Instead, he bristled, and unexpectedly he reversed the pressure:

'You are stating the obvious, Guy. But is that how you yourself have acted recently? You could have had my brother as a History Professor. What better way to bring our two subjects together? Instead, what do you do? You scrape around to find reasons to reject him.'

Guy Johnson was thrown back by this unexpected attack, the more so because it was at least plausible. He stalled, while he thought how best to respond.

'I can't think why you say that, Daniel. You don't know the reasons, only the outcome.'

'No. Because you took care never to give me the reasons.'

The Dean now had to make a decision. Should he finally reveal the full facts? Should he admit that if Michael Mellors had joined the History department the fear was that he might act as a 'spy' for English? Some men would have been sensitive enough to understand this fear and to allay it; but Michael Mellors had not revealed enough of his personality for the panel to be sure about him.

Meanwhile, the Professor of History was silent. He wanted to support the Dean, but he did not know what to say that would check Mellors.

The Dean's hesitation gave Mellors the opportunity to pile on the pressure.

'There can be no doubt that my brother was academically well qualified. Look what has happened since. He's been appointed to a chair at Manchester. A slap in the face for Blackchester!'

The Dean still stalled. 'So your brother's not suffered by being rejected by us.'

'No. But that was not the reason why you rejected him. You had no idea that he would get an offer from Manchester. I'm bound to suspect that your desire for better relations between History and English is at best qualified. It has to be on terms that favour History.'

The Dean was stunned that his attempt to bring History and English together had backfired into a personal accusation of prejudice. 'Nonsense. I'm surprised that you make such a charge.'

But he still did not go into detail about the rejection of Michael Mellors. He had decided that to reveal the truth about History's 'spy' fear would not calm Mellors down, quite the contrary.

Mellors made one final attack:

'I notice that you are saying nothing, Andrew. I take your silence to mean that you cannot deny the charge that in rejecting my brother History was being indulged. I suspect it is indulged in other ways.'

That was it. The Professor of English then swept out of the Dean's office without waiting for an answer. Guy Johnson's well-meaning attempt to encourage harmony between the two subjects had ended in disaster. Andrew Grey was left to talk over with the Dean the consequences, if any, of this spat:

'Well, Guy, where are we now? Is there anything more that you can say or do that would calm Daniel down? I fear not.'

'No. Nothing. We have to hope that he settles down of his own accord. If he does not repeat this complaint to anyone else we can carry on regardless.'

But characteristically the Professor of English did not remain silent. He spoke bitterly to his English colleagues, and to others in the Faculty.

'The historians are jealous of our progress, and the Dean has fed their jealousy. This latest conversation has confirmed that he is on their side. He was biased against my brother. And so were Andrew Grey and Adam Thwaite, both on the panel. Of course they had to go through a charade of seeming to take my brother seriously. They got away with it in the short-term. But now this Manchester appointment has made Blackchester look foolish in the eyes of the academic world.'

This last point began to circulate widely on campus. Even the scientists talked about it. It seemed to prove that Guy Johnson and the historians had blundered. Why had they never fully explained themselves? Was it because they dare not do so?

Daniel Mellors decided to exploit his new-found support. He had lost patience with Guy Johnson. After talking to his friend the Professor of French, he framed a motion to be put to Faculty Board. It was cleverly phrased so as to make tacit reference to the Manchester appointment. It sounded temperate, but was not: 'In retrospect, the board regrets that no appointment was ever made to the new chair of Modern History.'

If the Dean simply refused to accept this motion, Mellors indicated in conversation that he would complain to the Vice Chancellor. Even if the Dean accepted the motion – and yet during discussion at the board continued to refuse to explain why Michael Mellors had been rejected – the Professor of English intended to complain. In short, Guy Johnson was exposed either way.

What should the Dean do? Mellors had now begun to hint that Guy Johnson was losing the confidence of the English board. If such critical feeling solidified, Johnson would be bound to resign, for he would have lost the support of the largest subject in his Faculty. He consulted the Professor of History:

'This is very serious, Andrew. Daniel has moved on from the particular to the general – from asking about his brother to asking about my competence. I have to take this seriously.'

'Yes, Guy, I understand that. But don't let him rush you.'

The Professor of History sounded out his colleagues informally, in particular Adam Thwaite, who had been on the interviewing panel and so was well qualified to comment. To Grey's surprise, Thwaite was not entirely supportive of the Dean:

'We both know that Guy is a good Dean. But that is not where the present upset now centres. Daniel has chosen different ground. We have to consider how the argument appears to observers from the outside – say, to a lecturer in physics. We did seem to take a long time after Richards dumped us for Bristol. It became known that Michael Mellors was in the frame. Yet we stalled and eventually rejected him. Guy – for good reasons – has always refused to explain why – the 'spy' dimension. Alas, that looked suspicious at the time, and it has looked even more suspicious now that Michael Mellors has been thought worth the Manchester chair.'

'You think so?'

'I do. It's all a matter of appearance from the outside. Thanks to the Manchester appointment Daniel was given a chance to reopen the whole business, and he has made the most of it.'

Andrew Grey knew that if someone as experienced and sensible as Adam Thwaite was thinking like this, the Dean might indeed have to resign for the sake of peace in the Faculty.

The Dean himself began to sense the way things were going. He decided to bring the issue to an immediate head. He did so by sending a clear negative to the request from the Professor of English for discussion at Faculty Board of the History chair question. He sent copies to all board members: 'I cannot allow discussion at Faculty Board of the proceedings of the Modern History chair panel. The proceedings of such bodies are always treated as confidential. The name of any successful candidate is of course announced, but not why they have been appointed. Their reputation is left to speak for itself. If no one is appointed that decision may remain simply as a fact, without any obligation to explain why.'

As threatened, the Professor of English now requested an interview with the Vice Chancellor. Yet ominously his covering note did not even mention the History chair question as such. Instead, his language was now much broader. He wanted 'to discuss the position of English within the Arts Faculty'.

The Vice Chancellor read this request with concern. He was of course well aware of the rivalry between the Professors of History and English, and also of the tension caused by the rejection of Michael Mellors. But the VC was surprised to find that this had expanded into a threat to the future of the

Dean. Before seeing Daniel Mellors, he therefore invited Guy Johnson to comment:

'Mellors does not mention you by name, but the Registrar tells me that English (and perhaps also French) now want you out. What do you make of this? How have things suddenly gone so far?'

'I think I can explain why it has all come up now. It was the appointment of Michael Mellors to a chair at Manchester, which gave his brother the chance to re-open the whole question of Michael's rejection by us. Daniel has done so adroitly, and made it the subject of much gossip within and beyond our Faculty. The details of the panel's discussions are still not known to outsiders; but the defects or otherwise of Michael Mellors are no longer central. It has become a broader question of my conduct as chairman of the panel, and beyond that of my conduct as chairman of the Faculty. The charge has now surfaced that my handling of Faculty business has demonstrated that I always favour History.'

'I see. Is there any truth in the charge?'

'None at all. I find Mellors more difficult to humour than Andrew Grey, the History Professor; but I allow for that. Grey feared that if Michael Mellors were appointed to the History chair he might act as a "spy" for English among the historians. I saw the point of that, especially as we found it difficult to assess Michael's personality. There was no doubt about his ability. We pondered for several days, hence the delay for which we are now being blamed. But rejection was the safe option.'

'What do you want me to say to Mellors?'

'Well. I cannot stay as Dean on some sort of probation, required to prove my impartiality. I can only remain in post if Mellors, on behalf of English, withdraws his charge. If he refuses, he must understand that he is forcing my resignation.'

'I understand your logic, Guy. But is it always prudent to be logical?'

'Oh, I will go with real regret. The Faculty has a great future. Whether I stay on as Professor of Classics remains to be seen. Only let it be clearly known that I resign not because I admit to having favoured History, but for the sake of peace in the Faculty.'

The Vice Chancellor spoke to the Professor of English next morning:

'You do not mention Guy Johnson in your note, but I understand that your concern relates to him.'

'I fear it does. The English board suspects that he favours History, and believes that his conduct of the History chair business confirms this. Otherwise my brother would have been appointed.'

'What evidence do you have?'

'Circumstantial. My brother has been thought worth a chair at Manchester, and yet Guy Johnson flatly refuses to explain why he was rejected here. Beyond that, I've never had the Dean's ear, whereas the Professor of History always gets a hearing. Until now, I've tolerated such unfair treatment, and lived with it.'

The Vice Chancellor might have urged Daniel Mellors to think again, but he sensed that things had gone too far. Mellors would not now simply climb down. The last hope was to find out how much support English had within the Faculty.

'Is English on its own in making this complaint?'

'Oh no. I've spoken to the Professor of French. He backs me. I've not spoken to German or Italian, but they often go with French. Philosophy is too wayward to predict.'

'The Dean has said that he will resign if you do not immediately withdraw your charge – even though you've not made it explicit. He says he will go for the sake of peace in the Faculty.'

This was of course the decisive moment, and both men knew it. Mellors came up with a formula which was scarcely a compromise:

'I will not press my point if Guy promises to be impartial in the future.'

This of course would have left Guy Johnson admitting by implication that he had been partial in the past. Nonetheless, the Vice Chancellor felt bound to test the Dean's reaction at a further meeting:

'I've spoken to Mellors, Guy. I pressed him to climb down. But I fear he has gone too far in public to do that totally. The best I could get out of him was a promise to say no more (and I quote his words) "if Guy promises to be impartial in the future".'

'Oh, I can't live with that, as I think he realises. He wants me out. Given his now open hostility, I'm now sure that I ought to go.'

'It will look bad outside, Guy, just when we're starting to make an impact. You are thought to be a good Dean of a lively Faculty. People in other universities will ask why this upset has occurred, and will no doubt get garbled answers.'

'I see all that, Vice Chancellor. But my position within the Faculty has been damaged beyond repair.'

There was really little more to say. Guy Johnson slept on what to do, but did not change his mind. He spoke to Andrew Grey, who reluctantly agreed that for the sake of peace there was now no choice for Johnson but to step down. It was significant that Grey soon moved on to practicalities:

'If you must resign, Guy, you cannot do so instantly. Leave us time to find a successor. Meanwhile keep things going. Remain in post until the end of the academic year.'

And that was what happened.

(4)

The mechanics of Johnson's resignation proceeded smoothly enough. Enquiries were made confidentially in the university world about possible candidates; and an advertisement appeared in the usual newspapers. Externally all was well. But unfortunately, not everything was destined to run equally smoothly on campus.

Teaching proceeded as normal in the Arts building, with dozens of young people coming and going to lectures, seminars or tutorials. The busiest time was around each hour. Against this crowded background, the paths of the Professors of History and English were bound to cross sooner or later. As it happened, they did so outside the Arts lecture theatre only a few days after the Dean's decision to resign.

Daniel Mellors had just given a lecture, and was walking out: Andrew Grey was waiting to go in. Mellors had overrun his lecture time by some ten minutes, and this was what sparked the confrontation. Lectures were supposed to finish by five minutes before the hour, to allow time for student audiences to come and go.

Grey was annoyed: 'Overflowing with words as usual, Daniel.'

Mellors bristled: 'What do you mean, "as usual"? I use words to tell the truth. I realise you don't like words of truth when they don't suit you.'

'What do you mean? That I'm a liar?'

'I recall that you and the Dean have leaned over backwards not to tell the truth about my brother.'

Both men had coloured visibly. Mellors was blocking the door: Grey tried to make his way in, seeking to pass on Mellors's left side. Did he push his rival aside deliberately? Mellors thought so, and pushed back. Grey fell to the ground, surrounded by students, both History and English. Two History students helped him up. He had fallen heavily on to his elbow and was obviously in pain. All the History students saw this, and surged forward into the doorway in anger. The Professor of English was forced back into the block of English students who had been waiting behind him to quit the lecture theatre. The noise was now considerable, with most of the students shouting.

Attracted by the uproar, the Arts-block porter hurried over from his lodge. He was a retired sergeant-major. He found the two Professors glaring at one another, surrounded by noisy students, with the History Professor dishevelled and only just back on his feet. The porter took charge.

'Gentlemen, please!'

He saw that Grey's right arm was bleeding. 'Professor Grey, you're hurt. Let's get you to hospital.'

These words of common sense calmed things down rapidly. But much more was bound to result from this confrontation. The History secretary, who had been nearby in her office, immediately rang the Dean's secretary to report that the two Professors had 'come to blows'. The Dean's office was some distance away in the registry block, so he had heard nothing. He hurried over to the Arts building. Students were still milling around in the foyer, obviously over-excited. He went to talk first to the History secretary, who told him that the Professor of History had just been taken to hospital in Adam Thwaite's car.

'I don't think his arm is too badly hurt. At least, the porter who rescued him thinks not. But it needs x-raying to be sure.'

'You say "rescued". What on earth was going on? Who was attacking him?'

'I'm not sure, Professor Johnson. I wasn't there. I don't want to repeat gossip. George, the porter, will know more.'

So the Dean went next to the porter in his lodge.

'George, I gather you played a key role in settling things down. Thank you for that. But what was happening? Why were the two Professors coming to blows?'

'I didn't know why at the time; but I've gathered since that it was something to do with Professor Mellors being ten minutes late ending his lecture. It made Professor Grey angry, and words were exchanged, which became more than just words. Both had dozens of their students behind them.'

While Andrew Grey was being treated in the accident department of the local hospital, Daniel Mellors had retired to his office, visibly shaken but unhurt. He was talking over what had happened with his departmental secretary.

'I knew he was tricky. I didn't know he was violent. Get me some black coffee, please, Joyce, double quick.'

The Dean decided not to speak to Mellors straightaway. He felt that that the VC, rather than himself, should interview and reprimand the two Professors – partly because they were senior figures within the university and partly because the Dean knew that he was himself caught up in the coldness between the two men by allegedly favouring the History Professor.

Guy Johnson walked back to the VC's office, which was in the same building as his own. Fortunately, the VC was available.

'Ah, Guy, I've been trying to contact you. What's this about a fight between Mellors and Grey? Heaven help us! Was it really a fight?'

'I don't know much, Vice Chancellor. Something to do with Mellors being ten minutes late finishing his lecture, meaning that Grey was left waiting. It all happened in the lecture theatre doorway. But precisely what was said and done I don't yet know. Only that there were dozens of History and English students present. They became part of the confrontation. It's all very bad for the good name of the Faculty and the university.'

'Indeed it is.'

'I fear, however, that we cannot hush it up completely. Grey's at the hospital, and that will have been noticed. We'll have to admit something. The press will get on to it, and quiz the students.'

'Yes. Do we try to minimise things by saying something in advance, or do we wait and see?'

'We can't say that absolutely nothing happened. Yet we don't want to admit more than we have to. So best to wait and see what is said. We can react to that. There will be exaggerations, and we can play those down to good effect.'

'Yes. That's a shrewd point. We can take some of the wind out of their sails.'

The news duly broke in that evening's local paper. Its editor had tried to contact the Vice Chancellor, but had been told that he was not available until the next morning. Of course that did not prevent a reporter talking to students on campus. His report duly appeared on the front page:

PROFESSORS COME TO BLOWS

> Trouble flared this morning on the campus of Blackchester University. *But not between students.* Dozens of English students were coming out of a lecture theatre, headed by their Professor, and an equal number of History students were trying to get in, headed by their Professor. Neither side would give way. It is said that History Professor Andrew Grey tried to push English Professor Daniel Mellors aside. Mellors pushed back and Grey fell to the ground and struck his elbow. Porter George Rogers (53), a former sergeant-major, who stands no nonsense even from Professors, broke up the confrontation, and sent the Professor of History to hospital. So far the university has said nothing. Why? Parents will expect an explanation.

By the time the evening paper came out, the Professor of History had been delivered home from hospital, bruised and bandaged but with no bones broken. So he read the story in his own copy of the paper. His wife, who was usually so self-effacing, dared to ask if the report gave a fair account:

'If it is, you seem to be most to blame. What on earth were you doing? I know you don't like him, but why this?'

Grey brushed her questioning aside, but he realised that it was becoming a matter of 'who pushed who and why'.

Meanwhile the Registrar had taken a copy of the paper to the Vice Chancellor.

'Here it is, Vice Chancellor. It appears to target Andrew Grey most. You will of course have to hear his explanation as soon as you can – even though he's injured.'

'Yes. I must see them both as soon as possible. With Grey first, since he seems to be the main culprit. Of course, he may argue otherwise. '

The VC would have preferred to act that very evening; but he realised that Grey would still be shaken, first by what had happened and then by his hospital treatment. So he let the Professor of History have a night's sleep first.

The VC cleared his diary for the whole morning: he was determined to get on top of events. It had now become a national news story, fed to the Fleet Street papers by the Press Association. The *Daily Express* gave the fullest account, filling out its report with moralising about academics setting a bad example to the younger generation: 'Are our daughters safe in such places?' it asked. On first sight this was an over-reaction to a fracas between two Professors, bad though that was. But had the paper found out something else? Had it finally dredged up some old gossip about the Tom Tongue business? The VC read the article and wondered. He feared that, if so, and if the story developed in the press, the damage to the university's reputation would become much worse.

(5)

Andrew Grey was summoned to the Vice Chancellor's office for nine-thirty. The Dean was present, but had arranged with the VC to be there only as an observer. The VC led the conversation.

'I'm seeing you first because reports suggest that you were the prime mover in what happened. Do you agree?'

'It depends how you define "prime mover", Vice Chancellor. I was certainly the person who complained to Daniel Mellors about his lecture over-running by as much as ten minutes. I did so to his face.'

'What did you say?'

'I can't remember exactly. But it was something about Mellors being too fond of words.'

'What did he say?'

'He said that I was myself too ready to use words improperly. I asked if he meant that I was a liar. He said that the Dean and I had avoided telling the truth about his brother's application for the History chair.'

'Unpleasant. But not sufficient reason for a fight.'

'No. But it was never a fight in the sense of fisticuffs. I decided not to answer his charge. Instead, I tried to get past on his left side into the lecture theatre. There wasn't much room, and I brushed his left arm. But I was in no way pushing him. However, he reacted as if I were. He thrust out his left hand and sent me to the ground. I found that I had fallen awkwardly on my right elbow. Hence the injury.'

'Let me get this clear. There are two crucial points. First, that he called you a liar, even if he did not actually use the word. And second, that (even so) you did not intend to come to blows, and touched him only unintentionally while trying to get into the lecture theatre?'

'Correct. I was the innocent party throughout.'

'I understand there were lots of students behind each of you.'

'Oh, yes. Quite a mob. English behind him and History behind me.'

The VC decided that he had heard enough from Andrew Grey for now.

'Right. I have your outline. That's enough for a start. I

must now hear what Daniel Mellors has to say. I may talk to you again later this morning. After that, the university will probably issue a statement to the press. We would like to say nothing, but that may not be possible.'

Daniel Mellors was called in at ten-thirty. Before then the VC and Dean talked over Andrew Grey's account.

'Far from being the guilty party,' remarked the Dean, 'he seems to think he's the innocent party.'

'Yes. Foolish of him to try to push in at that point, but not violent.'

'So do you think that the blame shifts more to Mellors?'

'Possibly. Mellors made the verbal attack upon Grey and yourself. He then made the physical attack. Of course, he will claim that it was in self-defence. Let's see.'

'Yes, Vice Chancellor. But I cannot be present to hear Mellors since he thinks I'm biased against him. And he seems to have said so again. My presence might upset him further.'

So the VC saw Mellors one-to-one.

'I now have Andrew Grey's account of what happened. Obviously, I must hear yours. We need not waste time agreeing that this encounter should never have happened. But what precisely did happen?'

'My lecture ran late, and when I got to the door I found Andrew Grey standing there, with a mob of History students behind him. He said something about me being too fond of words. I said I only used words to tell the truth, unlike him. I said the Dean and himself had concealed the truth about their failure to appoint my brother to the History chair.'

'A pity that you dragged that up again.'

'Maybe. But it's true. And my words did not give him any excuse for violence. Instead of answering, he tried to push me aside. I pushed him back in self-defence. Not all that hard, but unfortunately he seems to have tripped and fallen awkwardly.'

'So the first push came from him?'

'Oh, yes.'

'And your push was not all that hard?'

'I was very surprised when he fell.'

'So you're the innocent party?'

'Yes.'

The Vice Chancellor smiled uneasily. 'Well. We seem to have two innocent parties. And no one guilty. I don't think there's going to be much point in me measuring blame. I will say no more than that I think both of you were very foolish. You have both allowed the rivalry between your subjects to get out of hand. You may not like one another, but in future you must work together regardless.'

The Professor of English looked as if he wanted to respond, but didn't. So the Vice Chancellor continued. 'I will say exactly the same thing to the Professor of History. Then I shall talk to the Dean about what to admit to the newspapers. Have you any suggestions there?'

'I suppose we must say something. Keep it short.'

'Yes. We can play it down if it's just a matter of a confrontation at the doorway. But Guy Johnson has spotted something in the *Express* which makes him wonder if there's been a leak about Tom Tongue.'

The VC then showed Mellors the cutting. They agreed that the paper's remark about daughters at the university might mean something or nothing. They could only wait and see.

Mellors returned to his office, while the VC called the Dean back to talk about a statement to the press. They agreed to say as little as possible as briefly as possible:

> Reports circulating in the press about an encounter on campus between the Professors of English and History at Blackchester University are much exaggerated. Both Professors accept that it was an unfortunate accident, which of course they much regret.

The editor of the local evening paper had asked a second time for an interview with the Vice Chancellor, but was told that it was not necessary. The goodwill of his paper was however useful to the university, and as a consolation prize he was given first use of its press release. So this appeared in his paper that same evening, but not in the national dailies until the next day, where its calculated feebleness ensured that it was lost within the inside pages.

So the damage to the good name of the university had been contained. Or had it?

The Registrar heard that a reporter from the *Daily Express* had come for a second time to the campus, and was asking students about Tom Tongue. Surely Tom's resignation was old news. But the *Express* report had hinted at a muckraking concern for standards of morality at British universities. If this concern surfaced in connection with Tom Tongue, it could still prove very uncomfortable for Blackchester.

On his second visit the reporter quizzed the students more about the past than about the present clash between the Professors. Eventually he found a third-year English student in Wells who, like Mary Parker, lived in Sheffield. The student knew her only by sight. At Easter 1955 he had seen her in Sheffield city-centre obviously pregnant. His surprise had made the student curious. When a week later he returned to the university he found that she had left in January. He told the reporter all he knew.

'Then last October I discovered that she'd come back. I assumed that she'd had the baby and left it at home with her parents. When our paths crossed by chance in a corridor I spoke to her for the first time. I ought to have said nothing, but instead I asked, "How's the baby?" And at this, she burst into tears and ran away.'

The reporter's ears pricked up, for he was beginning to sense a story.

'Who's the father? Another student?'

'I tried to find out. I spoke to a History student, a third-year like me. I know him quite well. He said he'd noticed she was back, but hadn't spoken to her. The story was that she'd been ill, but of course I knew otherwise. I told my friend I'd seen her pregnant, and that intrigued him. He said he'd ask around among the historians.'

'And what happened next?'

'He told them that he'd now heard for a fact that she'd been pregnant. Several of them then said they'd always thought there was "something fishy" about her leaving. She has a friend, Joan Peters, but when pressed Joan has always covered up – claiming that Mary suffers from a chronic illness. Until now that's been the story.'

The reporter wanted more.

'So there's been a cover-up. Who might the father be? Is that the reason for the secrecy?'

'I suppose so. But would they try so hard if the father is a student? The pair of them could have married, which would have deflated the whole story. Is it because the father is not a student?'

The reporter now began to be really interested. 'Someone on campus who is not a student?' he asked. 'Could it be a member of staff?'

Neither man asked the obvious alternative question – was the father some non-university person from Sheffield? This oversight was fortunate, for it kept them concentrating to good purpose upon the campus.

The *Express* reporter shrewdly narrowed the possibilities:

'Most likely to be one of her teachers. Who were her teachers in the term she became pregnant?'

'I don't know, but my friend in History probably will know. We could find him.'

'Good. If the paper makes a story out of this I'll see you get paid.'

The two men eventually found the friend going into the

Wells refectory, where they joined him for lunch. Two names emerged from their conversation: Richard Corke, who had been Mary's supervisor, and Tom Tongue.

The trio began to get excited:

'Richard Corke committed suicide.'

'When?'

'Last year, some time.'

'What official reason was given?'

'I forget.'

'Was there an inquest?'

'Yes, I think so.'

'Fine. We'll be able to check that. What was he like?'

'Well thought of. His suicide was a great surprise. Though afterwards people did say that he had no particular friends. Never a girlfriend. All things to all people.'

The reporter turned to the reputation of Tom Tongue.

'Is Tom Tongue more likely? A known womaniser, you say.'

'Yes. There was an upset some time ago about him and a young History lecturer, Tanya Jenkins. She objected to his attentions. She bit him when he tried it on. And he couldn't conceal his injury. It was a bit of a joke on campus. It all eventually died down.'

They agreed, however, that Tom's name had never been linked with that of a student:

'Perhaps it was bound to happen sooner or later.'

The reporter of course wanted not just suspicion but firm evidence:

'Are there any clues? Perhaps not direct but circumstantial.'

'Well, he later resigned. Said to have been given a visiting professorship for a year in Canada.'

The reporter, himself a graduate, was sharp enough to spot a possible weakness in this story:

'You say it was a visiting post. Why then did he not just take a year's leave? Why did he cut himself off from Blackchester by resigning?'

The two students of course did not know. But they agreed that it did not sound quite right. Was Tom Tongue being deliberately removed from the university? And if so, why?

There was no more for the two students to tell, so the reporter bid them a warm goodbye, and phoned his newsroom.

'My nose tells me he got this girl pregnant. He was her lecturer. I assume we want to expose him. We can link it all to our present story about the two Professors. And then rumble the whole university. We must take soundings in two places: in Sheffield where the girl lives, and in the Canadian university to which Tom Tongue has fled.'

A local reporter soon caught up with the Parker family in Sheffield. He did not contact Mary's parents directly. Instead, he made enquiries among neighbours on the road. They confirmed that she had indeed been pregnant. However, they also revealed that there was no baby for him to photograph because she had miscarried. Nobody knew who the father was, or if there had been a marriage. But no man had been seen. So the father was presumably not local. The reporter decided not to alert the Parkers at this stage by trying to interview them.

In Canada, enquiries soon confirmed that Tom Tongue was there as a visiting Professor. He had made himself popular at the university, but no one could say if he would be staying longer than a year. In other words, there was no certainty about his future across the Atlantic despite his resignation from Blackchester.

A few days later the *Express* reporter returned to the campus for a third time. He was now ready to press hard and to wind up. This meant meeting Mary Parker, preferably on her own. He intended not to ask if Tom Tongue was the father, but boldly to assume that he was.

The reporter enquired after Mary in the Wells refectory,

and eventually found someone who knew her room number. He had taken care not to draw attention to himself by asking the Wells porter about her. He knocked on Mary's door, and she opened it. His approach was cunning:

'Hello. My newspaper's doing an article on Blackchester as a new university – what being "new" actually means. I'm talking to lots of students, and someone has mentioned you.'

Mary's response was negative but not dismissive, for she did not realise the danger. 'I can't think why you've chosen me. I was away most of last year.'

This of course left room for the reporter to ask why. She gave her stock reply: 'Oh, I was ill.'

The reporter now moved in for the kill, using shock tactics covered in kind words:

'Yes, I was sorry to hear about your miscarriage.'

They were still standing in the doorway, and Mary staggered back.

'I don't think we'll need to mention anything about the miscarriage in our article.'

Mary looked slightly relieved, not noticing that this restraint did not cover the pregnancy itself. The reporter took his chance:

'Shall I come in? You could tell me about the university.'

So in he went, and sat down on Mary's desk chair. Mary was still standing, but he waved her to another chair.

'Do sit down. I need your help.'

He started with deliberate caution, drawing her into conversation by asking harmless questions:

'When did you start here?'

'October 1953.'

'When Blackchester had just become a full university?'

'Yes.'

'Was it what you expected?'

'More or less.'

'You took History, and your moral tutor was Richard Corke. A pity about his death.'

'Yes. He was nice.'

'Did you get to know him well?'

The reporter was of course deliberately fishing in case their relationship had been extra-close, but he found nothing. 'No, not especially.'

'All your courses were History courses?'

Mary did not spot the trap.

'No.'

'So you're allowed to take non-History courses?'

'Yes, just one.'

The reporter chose to remain gentle for just a little longer.

'A good idea. Not to be too narrow. What did you choose?'

' "Politics in Modern English Literature".'

'Who teaches that?'

Mary began to be guarded:

'It isn't taught any more.'

The reporter would not be put off; instead, he suddenly revealed himself:

'No. I've heard about Tom Tongue.'

Mary jumped at this sudden mention of Tom's name.

'We know about the hushing-up. But we're not sure about how to mention it. We don't want to be critical of you, only of the university. We may be able to mention your experience without naming you. Only Tom Tongue.'

The reality of Mary's situation had suddenly become clear to her. She went very pale, but she sensed that she was being offered a deal. She realised that the reporter probably knew most of her story anyhow.

'I don't have anything to do with him now.'

'No. I know about him being forced to resign. You could have covered things up by marrying the man.'

'He didn't care for me enough.'

The reporter became genuinely sympathetic.

'Well, we don't need to go into that. I'm only interested in the university angle. I don't want to press you about your feelings.'

The conversation ran on for another five minutes or so, during which time the reporter checked that he had got his facts right. Mary more or less confirmed that he had.

'Thank you, Mary. You've been very helpful. Difficult for you, I know. Fortunately, we won't need to mention your name.'

(6)

The reporter went back to London and filed his story. It appeared next day in a prominent position in the paper, accompanied by four photographs – one of the campus, plus one each of Tom Tongue and Professors Grey and Mellors:

MORE GOINGS-ON AT A NEW UNIVERSITY

In 1953 Blackchester University became a full university – no longer just a university college. Since then, parents have been sending their children there in the reasonable belief that their boys and girls would receive a good education from its professors and lecturers. But more than that – these same teachers have been expected to set a good example in their personal lives. In law, every university has a parental responsibility towards all students aged under twenty-one.

Yet what do we find? Readers will recall our recent report that two Blackchester Professors had fought each other at the entrance to a lecture theatre. The university did not deny this. It merely offered a feeble apology.

End of story? Not at all. We now find that recently there has been a much more serious instance of bad behaviour. This involved a student and a lecturer, and

> the university took great pains to hush it up. *We can now reveal the truth.*
>
> Tom Tongue, 41, a senior lecturer and a leading light in the English department, got one of his teenage pupils pregnant. He is a nationally-known Marxist, but whether Marxist free-love explains his behaviour we do not know. What is certain is that he refused to marry the girl. Instead, he has fled to a Canadian university.
>
> To keep things quiet, the Blackchester authorities allowed the culprit to resign rather than be dismissed. Dismissal would have cost Tom Tongue the Canadian job, but Blackchester was chiefly interested in protecting its own skin. It would have had to reveal the reasons for Tom's dismissal.
>
> Our two reports are connected. The guilty Marxist lecturer and his student victim came respectively from the English and History departments. So too did the pair of pugnacious Professors. Two departments at war?
>
> Little wonder that we are now asking if there is something rotten in the state of Blackchester?

The *Daily Express* was not much read by Blackchester academics, but it was the daily newspaper of the Vice Chancellor's secretary. In a state of shock she abandoned her breakfast and phoned the Vice Chancellor in his lodge.

'Vice Chancellor. Sorry to bother you so early. But have you seen today's *Daily Express*? It has a hostile article about Blackchester.'

'Hostile in what way?'

'It reveals everything about Tom Tongue.'

'The pregnancy?'

'Yes. The only thing it does not do is to name the student. It even brings in what it calls the two "pugnacious Professors". It ends by asking if there's "something rotten in the state of Blackchester".'

'Get Johnson, Mellors and Grey to my office at nine-thirty. Also the Registrar. Bring your own copy of the paper, but see if you can buy some more from the bookshop. If you get any phone calls from the press or BBC simply say that the university will be issuing a statement.'

The Dean and his History and English colleagues did not take the *Express,* and so knew nothing until they were phoned. To their growing discomfort, the VC's secretary read them extracts from the article. The Professor of History immediately phoned the Dean and they agreed to meet at nine o'clock, ahead of their meeting with the Vice Chancellor. The Dean rang the Professor of English and invited him to join them.

The Dean went straight to the heart of the matter:

'Our Faculty is of course to blame. No use pretending otherwise. What do we say to the VC? How do we minimise the impact on the university?'

'Frankly, I don't know,' answered Mellors.

'I haven't had time to think. A quick answer might be a wrong answer.'

Grey agreed: 'Yes. I'm stunned. We can't now deny that the pregnancy happened, although we must be careful not to reveal Mary Parker's name. I'd better talk to her as soon as possible, to find out how much she's been involved with the paper. I can't believe she would have spoken willingly.'

The Dean's secretary therefore phoned the Wells hall porter, who found that Mary was in her room. The porter asked her to go to Professor Grey's office straightaway. She had not heard about the *Express* article, and so Grey quickly filled her in.

'How much did you know about this, Mary? I can't believe you wanted it to come out.'

'Oh no. I was shocked. But this reporter seemed to have found out most of the facts before he came to me. I didn't know what to say. He talked me into a sort-of deal. I reluctantly confirmed the story. In return, he promised not to reveal my name. At least, he seems to have kept his promise.'

'Yes. So far. But you must be very careful, Mary. Let me know if you're contacted again, and say nothing. Except that you're taking legal advice. That will check them.'

The five men duly met at nine-thirty, the VC in charge.

'This is of course bad, very bad. How do we react? We have to agree a response. Of course, it's all the fault of your Faculty, Guy, but the whole university is damaged.

The Dean had to accept the Faculty's guilt.

'We cannot now deny the fact of the pregnancy, or that some sort of fracas took place between you two outside the lecture theatre.' He waved his hand towards Grey and Mellors. 'That story would have died a death by now, if the pregnancy had not been finally discovered. As a result, the two things have been brought together as evidence for a seriously threatening charge against us all – that the university is not a fit place for young people.'

The Dean knew his Shakespeare well, and expanded the newspaper's quotation: '"To what issue will this come? Something is rotten in the state of Denmark."' The VC took up the discussion:

'Thank you for reminding us of Shakespeare's leading question, Guy. Yes, we start from *Hamlet.* What do we say? I suppose we could say nothing at all, and try to ride out the storm. But I doubt if the Council would buy that, even if we did. I've already had the chairman, Charles Ongar, on the phone. His butler had shown him the article!'

After some minutes of rambling discussion, a tone of despair mixed with irritation was setting in. Then Andrew Grey came up with a bright idea:

'We're going to find it hard to say anything effective right now. But we could always buy time. We could put out a statement simply saying that the matter has been referred to

Council. It's not meeting for four weeks. By then the novelty of the paper's attack would have been lost.'

A desperate reaction maybe. A Dunkirk evacuation. But no one could suggest anything more effective in defence of the university. So the VC eventually accepted the proposal:

'I will of course have to make an explanation to Council; so when we've had more time to think, we must meet again to discuss what I might say there. By then we'll know if the *Express* has anything further to add. I guess it will have. We must brace ourselves. In the meantime we can simply tell friend and foe alike to wait for the Council meeting. I can even say the same at Senate.'

Unsurprisingly, the refusal of the university to admit to anything gave the *Express* an excuse for anger:

> Blackchester is a public institution. It takes Government money. Yet when charged with serious misconduct it delays giving an answer. We can only assume that it has no defence to offer. It simply hopes that the problem will go away. But it won't. Tom Tongue, who fathered a student's child, may have been sent packing; but the two Professors who came to blows in front of their students are still in place. *Should they be? They may be bright in their subjects, but they are not bright in their behaviour. Are they suitable models for our children? We doubt it.*
>
> Let us remind you of their names – ***Andrew Grey***, Professor of History: ***Daniel Mellors***, Professor of English.

The two men of course read this renewed and very personal attack with horror. It was more direct than ever. It looked as if the paper wanted to do more than have the university scrutinised and cleaned up – the *Express* wanted them out. Could they resist such a campaign?

The follow-up article appeared in the *Express* a week after the first article. Andrew Grey was now taking the paper daily, and so read the attack at breakfast time. He pushed aside his corn flakes. As soon as he reached the campus he went to the Dean.

'They want my blood, Guy. What does the university say or do?'

The Dean read the article twice, obviously thinking hard. His sympathy was not unqualified:

'Yes, as you say. They do want blood. So I wonder if some slight blood-letting would be the clever answer. Not of course dismissal. But if you and Daniel were to be reprimanded by Senate at its meeting next week, the university could claim that it had acted positively.'

Grey was surprised by this suggestion, but reluctantly saw the Dean's point.

'Oh, well. Maybe. I don't know. We must find out first what Daniel Mellors thinks.'

So they spoke together to the Professor of English later that morning. 'I would need to see the form of words. I don't see why I should be blamed. I accept that things got out of hand, but the prime mover was Andrew here. It would not have happened but for him.'

This was of course true, so far as it went; but the Dean realised that some gesture was needed from the university:

'Yet we do need something. Suppose I see if I can concoct a mild motion of censure for Senate, which both of you can accept, even though reluctantly. If such a motion then stifles this worrying attack upon the university as a place of education, we would have served the greater good.'

The two Professors nodded guardedly but did not speak, so the Dean continued.

'As you know, the VC has passed to Council the broader charge – the charge against the university. But Senate can of course still reprimand its members, and such a reprimand would be reported to Council.'

By later that day Guy Johnson had composed a draft reprimand:

> Senate regrets that an encounter between the Professors of History and English has attracted recurring notice in the press. Senate believes that to make a detailed analysis of what happened would be unhelpful. It therefore simply expresses its regret that such an incident occurred, and its wish that nothing similar should occur again in the future.

The Dean was well pleased with this formula. He called back his two Professors and read out his words:

'I hope, gentlemen, you'll be ready to accept this reprimand. Neither of you is especially blamed. And after all, you do not deny that something happened, and to that extent you have already accepted a measure of responsibility.'

Andrew Grey spoke first.

'Yes. I suppose I can just about accept this … For the greater good. In the hope that it will stifle any broader attack upon the character of the university.'

Daniel Mellors sounded even more hesitant, but he nonetheless reluctantly acquiesced:

'Well … I suppose so … Of course, it leaves me admitting by implication to a guilt which I do not feel.'

Guy Johnson replied soothingly: 'That is unlikely to be noticed by the other faculties, Daniel. Even if it were, your generosity would be welcomed.'

This flattering gloss just about satisfied the Professor of English.

Senate duly passed this warning motion at its next meeting, with the Vice Chancellor not allowing any discussion. He rightly felt the less said the better, so the usual windbags were kept quiet.

Similarly, when Council eventually met, the VC communicated a very careful version of events. He emphasised the desirability of brevity, so that nothing might be said which could give the press any excuse further to rake things over. His words were therefore few and well chosen:

'None of the unfortunate facts revealed by the *Express* are disputable as such, so we did not dispute them when they were first revealed. What has mattered is the interpretation to be placed upon them. The *Express* has questioned the underlying moral character of the university. We have deliberately delayed saying anything about this general charge, while at the same time mildly censuring the two Professors for their particular actions. This policy seems to have worked. The wind has been taken out of the newspaper's sails.'

There were murmurs of agreement.

'At first, I thought we would need to issue a statement after this Council meeting. But now I think not. Any comment would be likely to attract counter-comment, so reviving the whole issue. I therefore recommend that we now simply pass on to other business.'

This was of course an unexpected proposal, but the chairman knew what was coming:

'Yes. I agree. I realise of course that many of you have comments to make. We have all been very worried for the university. Its future has been threatened. But think hard. What more can we say that it's wise to say? Mum's the word. Thank you, Vice Chancellor, for your careful report. I shall say nothing more myself. Let us move on to next business.'

In this way Council stopped itself from digging any deeper. Instead, the crisis was successfully buried in the existing hole. The two social scientists whose dangerously sharp minds had finally exposed the 'bite' business, professed to be almost pleased. 'At least,' they exclaimed, 'everyone's now heard of Blackchester. And at least they'll know we're not stuffy!'

8

Back to Square One

(1)

The summer of 1956 witnessed the end of Blackchester's third year as an independent university. The first two of those years had been promising, especially for English and History. English had attracted a much increased number of new students for October 1954, and more again for 1955, while History had made a big effort to follow suit. This expansion was chiefly the work of the two Professors of English and History, Daniel Mellors and Andrew Grey. Both Professors had embarked upon clever publicity campaigns. Through the BBC, the Historical Association and the *Manchester Guardian,* they had made Blackchester much better known. They were coming men.

But, alas, in the middle of this progress things began to go wrong. Eventually, the two Professors came to blows in front of large numbers of their own students. Such a confrontation was of course bad enough, and the two men were formally reprimanded by the university. But even more damaging had been the conduct of Tom Tongue, the senior lecturer in English. He was a lively figure, known throughout the university world and beyond. Unfortunately, his liveliness had begun to get out of hand. First there was his gory attempt to kiss Tanya Jenkins, a very junior lecturer in History, after a party at his house. The resulting 'bite' business had become the talk of the campus among staff and students alike, generating some smiles but much more disapproval. Tom tried to conceal what he had done, but failed. So far so bad for him and for the university. But much worse – even though known at first to very few – was Tom's non-love affair with a student. He had made Mary Parker pregnant, and yet he was hesitant about marrying her. His hesitation provoked his eventual rejection by Mary. This meant that there was to be no happy ending for the couple – quite the opposite, for the agony was given a new dimension when Mary eventually suffered a miscarriage.

The university's efforts to keep all this quiet appeared at first to have succeeded. Tom Tongue was discreetly removed from Blackchester, being allowed to take himself off to a post in Canada without public censure. But in the end the press found out what had happened, and the moral character of the new university came under sharp questioning. The *Daily Express* in particular asked if Blackchester was a fit place in which to educate young people, especially young women?

The university authorities handled the situation with some skill. They did not deny the facts – when these had become undeniable; but they carefully said the minimum in reply, and let time pass. This dead-bat policy worked up to a point. The attacks petered out.

Many schoolteachers were *Express* readers, and large numbers of them now decided to play safe. Whereas previously they had started to recommend Blackchester to their pupils as a place to consider, after reading the bad news stories many teachers changed their minds: 'I'm not sure about that place after all, Smith. Try Leicester instead.' As a result, Blackchester's intake of English and History students fell back to its modest earlier totals.

So the worthy efforts of the two Professors had failed. They were left frustrated and very angry – even if not angry with themselves. Instead, they blamed Tom Tongue, and they blamed each other. They knew that they would have to start all over again. But would Andrew Grey ever be able to find another prime minister quite so ripe for discrediting as 'Mr Gladstone'?

And perhaps instead of starting again at Blackchester, the two Professors might do better to move to posts elsewhere. But their upsets had become known throughout academia. Would any other more prestigious universities be willing to rescue them? The two men had always intended to move on eventually; but they had expected to progress from a situation of personal success, not of embarrassing failure.

And what about the younger people at Blackchester? Fortunately, the outcome for them was much more positive. Among the staff, Tanya Jenkins was given her permanent lectureship in History, and completed her PhD. After a couple of years Dick Rogers left Blackchester for an Oxford fellowship. Among the students, Peter Proudfoot duly got his first-class degree, but he and Mary Parker drifted apart after graduation. They had been good for one another in different ways, but theirs had been only a campus romance. Mary achieved her upper-second, and contentedly became a schoolteacher. Her self-confidence towards the opposite sex had been sufficiently restored, and no doubt one day she would make a satisfactory marriage. She never wanted to see – or even to hear about – Tom Tongue again.

What then happened to our sexual predator? Was he given a permanent post in Canada? No. The Canadians caught up with his Marxist past, and he was forced to return to England after one year. Luckily for him, an English department with left-wing leanings eventually offered him a senior lectureship. After that, he slipped into an active middle-age, as sociable as ever. He was destined to play a prominent part in the street politics of the sixties, and not to die until past ninety. He then received an indulgent obituary in *The Times*, written by a Marxist professor, who called him a 'life force'. After Mary, there had been many further women in his life, but none, so far as is known, were university students. Likewise, he does not seem to have fathered any more children. On the other hand, he did father an aphorism. To the end of his days, he liked to repeat the same bold form of words in defence of sexual freedom on campus: 'Universities are places of learning: virginity is ignorance.'

(2)

Blackchester was trying hard to settle down. But did it succeed? Before long, a tasty new rumour began to circulate on campus. This hinted that Professor Grey's wife, Jennifer, was having an affair with the new Professor of American Literature, Geoffrey Boswell, a bachelor. Amazing. Yet surely this story could be dismissed as unbelievable. Everyone knew that Mrs Grey was rarely seen on campus, and that she was scarcely the type.

And yet in academia you never can be quite sure. People live so close together. The alleged lovers had of course first met when the Greys gave a dinner party at their home for the new Professor. Such a gesture reaching across subjects was rare. It had been meant by Andrew Grey to encourage the new man to feel more sympathetic towards History than his long-serving colleagues in English. Fair enough. But had the desired two-subject sympathy gone much further than the Professor of History intended?

The rumour was given more strength and colour when the Greys eventually announced that – after fifteen years of marriage without a pregnancy – they were expecting a child. This news attracted much more interest on campus than was usual with such a family event. Unsurprisingly, the two gossiping social scientists who had exposed the truth in the 'bite' business, were early on the case. This time their suspicion was expressed in coded language: 'I wonder,' they chuckled, 'if the baby will have an American accent.'

When Daniel Mellors, the Professor of English, first heard this slur, he blamed his rival, the supposed cuckold, as much as he blamed his English colleague, the alleged lover. Certainly, both departments found themselves greatly embarrassed. And yet they could do nothing about it. We have seen how Mary Parker's pregnancy had been terminated by a miscarriage; but no such upset was destined to trouble Jennifer Grey. On the contrary, in due time she gave birth to a bouncing baby girl.

The baby was born at home, and its arrival was soon being talked about on Blackchester's campus. In the SCR our two gossipy social scientists were predictably on hand to welcome the news.

'I wonder,' mused one of them mischievously, 'if the Greys will call the child "Unity".'

'Oh, yes,' answered his colleague, slyly underlining his friend's point by coining a damaging pun: 'There can be no doubt. After all, everyone knows she's been born into a Grey area!'